3-15-202

Life is
why ...
... one.

Enjoy!
B. B. Giesler

THE
BLIND
JUSTICE
SOCIETY

BB GIESLER

This book is dedicated to my husband William, who lost a courageous battle with pancreatic cancer on July 26, 2016. His strength, encouragement, and true love are in every story in this book. He would listen to me read to him during his chemo treatments. I can hear him saying you used too many she's, and the word said shows up too many times. Should I be afraid to sleep with you?

I love you, dear man. Thank you for my beautiful life. I miss you every day. I see you in our flower gardens and the birds that sing to me. The best of all is your watch chiming at noon every day. What's for lunch, you would say. You are my soulmate, and I will always love you.

Bonnie.

ACKNOWLEDGMENTS

My children, family, and friends whose gift of love and devotion to my dream prompted me to write this book. Their faith and support in my endeavors to finish this book even in my grief of the loss of my husband. My son Jon always referring to me as "Murder She Hopes." My son Josh whose character was killed in my first flash story. My daughter Jennifer who became the listener of my stories after my husband was gone. My beautiful grandchildren, nieces, and my crazy sister. Billy Ann went to anything I asked her to do. Even CSI training. My writing coach Nick better known as the Ripper. Thank you all. I am blessed and loved by a wonderful group of people.

CONTENTS

THE INTRODUCTION TO
THE BLIND JUSTICE SOCIETY

THE TAVERN

Harriet's tavern, from the front, looked rustic, humble, and intimate. The color-glass windows made it challenging to look inside. It had a view of the river and small coves that surrounded cabins. The regulars kept it busy and the summer crowd filled it every night. This quaint town provided residents and visitors water activities to keep them occupied. Sailing, swimming, jet skiing, kayaking, and paddle-boarding. Several sandy beaches, biking, and hiking trails.

Sadie, a part-time resident and her partner Nigel, entered the bar through the heavy metallic doors, greeted by the aromas of roasting food. Sadie took a moment to adapt her eyesight to the dim lighting. The bartender, Gina, struggled to get the orders out but acknowledged them with a wave.

Employees from the shipyard in their soiled clothes and sailors whose ships were in for repair work were the primary clientele this hour of the day, along with the locals. Groups occupied several tables where they had bonded over the superb cuisine, conversation, and happy-hour prices. They also occupied stools at the bar.

Sadie heard a recognizable voice calling her name.

"Sadie, over here!" yelled Ginny Adams, waving her hand, sitting at a table with several women from the neighborhood. The regular Friday happy-hour pitcher of margaritas was on the table and a glass waited for Sadie to join the sleuth group.

Ginny and some women from the neighborhood were amateur sleuths, or as the bar goers referred to them, the old biddies. Retired women, law enforcement, and lawyers made up the sisterhood. If they thought there was anything that appeared illegal, their noses were in it. Sadie found them fascinating and great storytellers. She also appreciated that amateur sleuths help figure out hundreds of the oldest and coldest cases in the country.

She and Nigel made their way to the table. "Hi, ladies."

"Sit over here," said Ginny. The women shifted position to make room. Nigel needed to lie on the floor next to Sadie. Ginny poured Sadie a margarita.

"Here's to the end of the week and Sadie's homecoming," said Ginny.

Sadie Barker was an undercover FBI agent. And Nigel was her partner, a muscled ninety-five-pound German Shepard guide dog. Whenever she got home, Sadie hung out with this group of women.

She picked up her glass and savored the first sip.

"So, what are you ladies up to?"

The women were chattering about how Ginny had proven the city manager was engaged in a crime, and she was the reason the police apprehended him. And how Audrey Chambers and her dog Harley discovered a financial corporation was cheating widows out of their spouses' retirement. They also solved the case of the husband who poisoned his wife. These women belonged to a group they had created called The Blind Justice Society. They selected that name because of Sadie and Nigel. The old biddies loved it.

Sadie was their leader. She was a special agent and had access to intelligence they might need. She had law enforcement friends and lawyers that belong to this society and knew many diverse women over the country. They didn't have organized meetings, but they knew how to contact each other. The members understood how to operate today's technology.

"Let's have another pitcher," said Ginny.

"It's on me," laughed Sadie.

Happy-hour on Friday was a tough time for a meeting or a discussion because of the commotion. The women laughed and chatted until they consumed the second pitcher. Karaoke night was beginning. It was time for them to go home and start their weekend. Sadie, Nigel, and Ginny left together. They lived near each other.

"Can you tell me about anything involving your last case?" asked Ginny as they strolled along the water.

"I can tell you the agency gave me another partner, along with Nigel. It was a complex and awkward assignment. He's a good-looking guy with a terrific sense of humor. Nigel liked him," Sadie chuckled.

"What a terrific case to have. Did you get the perps?" asked Ginny.

"We did. And I wish I could tell you more," replied Sadie.

"Here's my street," said Ginny. "See you tomorrow."

"Goodnight," said Sadie. She strolled to her condo and glanced out over the river and the gentle ripples in the water.

Tears of sorrow filled her eyes. Agent Sadie Barker in real life was having eyesight issues. It was ironic. She had been acting blind for years in her undercover position, and now this real eye disease could lead to a shift in her career.

At first, Sadie had become clumsy and bumped into objects. She had trouble seeing well in the dark. It hadn't interfered with her job yet, but Sadie knew it could jeopardize the safety of others. The only individual who knew all this was Ginny. She had noticed Sadie's clumsiness and, being a nurse, had figured it out. Ginny promised not to tell anybody, but she made Sadie promise she would inform her boss soon.

The time had arrived, and when Sadie returned to Washington D.C., she would tell her supervisor, Agent White, what was happening. If she didn't have eye surgery, the disease could take her eyesight. Her recovery could take three months. And there were no guarantees.

After her recuperation, Sadie wanted to return to her under-cover job. She wasn't confident the division would let her. This trip home was to concentrate on what she wanted out of life.

Nigel would go with her, no matter her decision. The Blind Justice Society always needed full-time members.

THE BOOKHOUSE

"I, Sadie Barker, do solemnly swear that I will support and defend the Constitution of the United States against all enemies, foreign and domestic; that I will bear true faith and allegiance to the same; that I take this obligation freely, with no mental reservation or purpose of evasion; and that I will well and faithfully discharge the duties for which I am about to enter. So, help me, God." It had been five years since Sadie stood at her graduation ceremony from the FBI training facility at Quantico, Virginia, and raised her right hand to say those words. She graduated at the top of her class as she'd done in high school and college. An all-star lacrosse player and marksmen in the rifle club, she earned a complete scholarship to an Ivy League college. A criminal justice major at the top of her class, she was invited to join the Federal Bureau of Investigation. Now for the first time, Sadie was on undercover duty with a new partner. She was anxious.

Her assignment: to expose the members of the Church of the Prophets, who appeared to be laundering money through their followers. Several agents tried. None of them figured it out. The agency recognized Sadie's extraordinary sense of figuring out cases. She called it What's out of the ordinary.

She moved into the residence across the street from the church with Nigel. Sadie was thirty, lanky and slender, with long brown hair. Nigel was an agile well-muscled ninety-five-pound German Shepherd who operated as her service dog. Her persona faked that she was blind. Nigel wore a service vest that contained state-of-the-art technology, along with a weapon. Sadie and Nigel had been observing the church for several weeks now.

There was some out-of-the-ordinary behavior from the male members of the church. Sadie wrote in one of her reports that she'd seen several men walking into the church with one color shopping bag and coming back out with different colored ones. What men walk around with shopping bags? Many large and heavy suitcases were in and out of the church. They rolled easily across the parking lot. Sadie felt confident this was a cash transfer, but she required further evidence to get a search warrant.

The Church of the Prophets members had been identified to have anti-American ideologies. The government had captured several members planning and plotting against the United States. They were known for donating vast amounts of money to radical groups, but the government had never prosecuted them. The agency hoped Sadie would be the one to do so.

Every morning, Sadie and Nigel would take their walk, trying to identify everything or anyone that might provide a clue to the money laundering scheme. They had run into several members, some friendly and others cold. The men were cool, and they didn't like the dog. Nigel felt the same. The fur on his back would rise up, his ears pointed forward whenever he was near them.

On one walk, Sadie noticed a man standing at the neighborhood book exchange house. The place was small, the size of a child's dollhouse. It contained used books the individuals of the neighborhood donated. A man was poking through them. That wasn't unfamiliar. But the man was Abraham, the head of the church.

Tall and middle-aged with a dingy beard that contained thick grey streaks and a jagged scar stretching across his right cheek, he was easy to recognize. Sadie had met Abraham when she first moved in. They had spoken many times during her walks. He had asked her if she had been blind since birth or lost her sight later in life. She explained that she was born with a disease that had taken most of her sight, but that she nevertheless saw shadows. Sadie explained they considered her legally blind. What Abraham didn't realize was her dark glasses concealed a camera, a computer, and a cell phone that understood voice commands. Her cane was both a weapon and a voice recorder.

Abraham selected a book and crossed the street. He and Sadie came together at the corner. "Good morning," he said in a friendly tone.

"Good morning," replied Sadie.

He asked how she could always identify him. She explained that she could identify his footsteps, how his shuffling his feet on the ground created an unmistakable noise.

As they strolled up the street together, they passed the entrance to the church. The side door opened, creating a squeaking noise that startled Nigel and Sadie. A tall young man with dark hair resembling Abraham stepped out and spoke to them.

"Hello," he said.

"Hi," answered Sadie.

"This is my son," replied Abraham.

They exchanged a few words and she excused herself and headed home. Something about what she had just encountered gave her a sense of uneasiness. This wasn't commonplace, and she couldn't get it out of her mind. Sadie would have to keep a tighter watch on the church.

A few hours later, several cars pulled up in front of the church. A tall, broad-shouldered young man with dark hair got out of his car. It was Abraham's son. He wandered over and gave a man in another car a book. The man gave him one too. This went on with all the vehicles. Then they all sped away. They never spoke a word to each other. Sadie realized it was a way to send messages. She would have to figure out what these books were and try to get her hands on one. Sadie needed to find out what these individuals were doing. She would have to be discreet since they realized her vision was too weak for her to read.

It was after midnight. The street was dark and vacant. Sadie dressed in black to blend in with the darkness. She snuck down the hill. The streetlights appeared dim. They gave off an eerie sense of supernatural flickering. Strange shadows and sounds echoed off the church, delivering a chill up her spine. She had left Nigel at the end of their driveway. Sadie needed to peek into the neighborhood book exchange house and scan the books there. Her mind raced and perspiration flowed down her forehead. Opening the small door to the book house, she scanned the books with her glasses, which took pictures of the titles. Rushing back over the street, she hustled up the small hill. Signaling Nigel, she continued up the driveway to the house.

She placed the chip from the camera into her computer and downloaded the information. Then she clicked the file and started reviewing the titles. Nothing out of the ordinary here. It would take nights to compare all this information. Sadie sent her boss a text message informing him what she was doing. His responded, *Be careful because the night has eyes.*

The weekend brought even more surprises. Sadie was enjoying her early morning coffee when an old beat-up truck pulled up in front of the church. It seemed familiar to her, but she couldn't place it. A slender, long-haired man dressed in a camouflage jacket and jeans got out. He strolled over to the side door of the church and punched in some numbers on the keypad. It didn't work. He tried repeatedly. He then sauntered up to the other building of the church and knocked on the door. No answer. He tried the windows on the first floor, even pulling on the air conditioners. He couldn't get in. Sadie started filming the man, thinking to herself, "Who breaks into a church?" As she observed him, she realized he had left a substantial plastic sack in the bed of his truck. A bomb?

Sadie panicked. What should she do now? Could she just ignore this? The man was speaking on his phone. Stomping back to his truck, he snatched the plastic sack and opened his truck door. He flung the door and walked over to the window of the structure. He held the plastic bag and a crowbar in his hand. The intruder started prying the window open. Sadie's mind raced. Three men occupied the second floor. Why had they not responded to the man's knocking? Buildings and homes surrounded the church. People could get injured or killed. She grabbed her phone. The man pried the window open. As his feet slipped inside the window, Sadie gave the street address to the police dispatcher.

"What the hell," she said.

Sadie grabbed Nigel and her service revolver. Before she could get out the door, police were all over the street. Sadie sighed an instant relief. She wondered if she had been the only one watching the church. Within moments, the police hauled the man out of the building and onto the ground. They searched him and the old beat-up truck. When the search was over, the police left. It confused her. There was a sudden hollow echo of knuckles knocking on the door. Sadie grabbed Nigel and put on her glasses.

"Who is it?" she asked.

"Sergeant Lewis. City Police," a deep voice replied.

She could see through the door window. A tall, broad-shouldered police officer stood waiting for her to open the door. Did he know her cover? Sadie opened the door with caution.

"I wanted you to know the man was here to paint the inside of the church."

Sadie's expression on her face must have looked bewildered.

"The church told him to break in. Also, you never called. We never had this conversion." He turned and left.

Sadie was confused and not clear if her boss would understand why she became involved. She closed the door and moved back to her tepid coffee. Nigel sat there, gazing at her. She patted the smooth silky fur on his back.

Sadie returned to the neighborhood book exchange house several times before she discovered what she considered substantial evidence on the money laundering. Two books kept showing up: The Bible and The Book of Mormon. Neither one of these books fit the church. She had identified different words and numbers underlined or highlighted. She decided the next time the books returned, she would take a set and see the reaction from the church members. Sadie contacted her boss about what she had found and what her intentions were. He didn't bring up the painter, but she was confident he knew. Maybe it had been a test.

Sadie went for a walk to clear her mind. This case was more complex than she expected it would be. Nigel and Sadie enjoyed all the manicured lawns and splendid flower gardens. As they turned the street to come around to the back of the church, she spotted several parked cars with out-of-state license plates. New Jersey, New York, Massachusetts, even Virginia. She walked by them, snapping detailed pictures of the automobiles. The last car's driver's window was down, and a cell phone was lying on the seat. Sadie grabbed it and copied the data. As she did it, she brushed against the car and the alarm went off. The loud beeping and honking was noisy and disruptive to the people praying in the church. Her heart raced, beating harder and harder. She panicked. "Come on!"

The phone beeped, and she tossed it back into the car. A heavy, grey-haired man appeared around the corner.

"What are you doing!" he yelled in broken English.

"I bumped the car and the alarm went off. I'm sorry," replied Sadie.

She gave Nigel a command and continued walking. Her glasses were like a rearview mirror, and she could see him searching his car. He scowled and watched her every step. Sweat poured down her brow. "That was close," she thought. "I should be more careful." Just the same it had been exciting.

She downloaded all the information she had collected from the cell phone and was astonished with what she had discovered. Sadie now recognized how they were laundering money. The cell phone information was part of a code.

Time for her boss and all the other agents to look over the information Sadie had found. Sadie contacted her boss and made plans for several agents to have dinner at the house. They all came around seven. Sadie and Nigel were on the deck barbecuing.

"What a marvelous place," Jeff said in his usual teasing manner.

Acting like old friends, the agents chatted for a while outside and then went into the house to eat. After dinner, they all gathered around the computer so Sadie could show them what she had found. The information that she had copied from the phone appeared on the computer screen. They wondered if they could trust that someone had left a phone on the seat of their car with this information, let alone leaving the window down. It seemed suspicious.

"Maybe it's a trap," Jeff said. "Continue working on getting the books. I consider that a necessary piece of the puzzle." The books they thought held more code and other answers that the team needed in order to make an arrest.

The next evening, Sadie visited the neighborhood book house. To her astonishment two copies of the books were in the book house. They weren't there two nights ago. She grabbed one of each and made her way back up the dark and eerie street. There seemed to be eyes scanning her like a predator. Like they were hunting her down. Sadie held her breath and rushed up the hill. She was out of breath and exhausted, going into the house and making her way with Nigel to bed. She would start working in the morning on the books with a sharp mind.

In the morning, after her walk, she examined the books, comparing what was different. She realized she wasn't getting anywhere, so she took a break. The deck was so inviting with wicker chairs and comfy cushions. Sadie and Nigel settled in and watched the sun sparkling off the water. The salty breeze was gentle and seagulls circled overhead, making sharp squawks that soothed her. Sadie drifted off to sleep.

Nigel growled, and Sadie woke up, startled. She recognized that she was unarmed. Her cane and a weapon were in the house. What a stupid thing to do.

The man from the car alarm walked up her deck steps. Sadie gave Nigel a command, and he listened but didn't move from her side. He was ready to do his job. All he needed was a signal.

"I'm sorry. He is my protector," Sadie said, trying to sound apologetic.

"I've seen you out walking with him," the man said in broken English. "I attend the church across the street."

"What can I do for you?" asked Sadie.

"I think you took information off my phone yesterday," he said.

"I don't understand," said Sadie.

"Yes, you do."

Had he seen as her copying information onto her phone? Did he have some kind of security on his phone she was not aware of? Sadie knew she was unarmed, but she had Nigel. He would kill if she gave him the command.

"I don't have a clue what you're implying," she snapped. "Get off my property or I will give my dog a command that will hurt you."

She moved her hand, and Nigel stood up with his head somewhat raised and showed his teeth with a growl that came deep from his throat.

"Do you need to see any more?"

The man reached in his pocket. Nigel growled, showing more teeth and edging toward the intruder. The man backed down the stairs. Nigel's growls grew milder. He stopped at the bottom of the stairs and glared at Sadie and Nigel.

"Tell whoever you're working for they shouldn't send a woman to do a man's job," he said in a chilling voice.

Sadie was shaken and furious at herself. She had left herself in a vulnerable spot outside on the deck. She called her boss.

"Special Agent White," he answered.

"Hi, it's Sadie."

"What do you need?" he said.

"I had a visitor. The gray-haired man. He said he knew I took something off his phone. Oh yeah, and he said don't send a woman to do a man's job."

Jeff laughed. "The crew will be over in an hour. You need to download and back up the files. Time to move on them."

The crew, as Jeff called them, arrived in an hour dressed as a carpet and floor cleaner. Sadie had everything backed up, downloaded, and packed. The plan was for her to stay the night with her surveillance cameras running and take a walk in the morning. If she ran into Abraham, she would tell him she was leaving on a vacation.

That night seemed extra-long for Sadie. She and Nigel had finished their first uncover assignment and had gotten the information the agency was seeking. Now what? The next morning, they took their usual walk. As if it was meant to be, they ran into Abraham.

They chatted, and Sadie told him, "Nigel and I are going on vacation for a few weeks."

"I hope you have a safe trip," Abraham wished her.

When Sadie was ready, she called a taxi. It arrived early and started honking in the driveway. She peeked through the surveillance camera. To her surprise, the driver was the grey-haired man. Also, she saw movement on the passenger's side on the ground. There were surveillance cameras on both sides of the driveway. It was the painter. They were there for Sadie. She tapped her glasses and activated the phone.

"I have company, and I don't think they're here for a cup of cappuccino."

"How many?" asked her boss.

"Two," she replied.

The driver kept honking and beeping.

She yelled down to the driver, "Could you help me with my suitcase?"

"Stand down," yelled Jeff.

"Too late."

Sadie was outside the door, pushing her suitcase over to the top of the stairs. Nigel was at her side. The man started up the stairs, checking to see if Sadie made any unusual movements. As he reached the top of the stairs, Nigel squatted down and urinated. Sadie bent down to pat him and took her pistol out of his service coat. As she lifted her hand, Nigel attacked. His massive body forced the man and him over the railing. They landed in front of the taxi. Nigel kept his mouth wrapped around the man's wrist. He was yelling in pain. The man on the side of the cab stood up, pointing a gun at Nigel.

"Put your weapon down," shouted Sadie from the deck.

She heard the gun cock. Without hesitation, Sadie fired. Still a sharpshooter. She ran down the stairs and over to Nigel. He was fine.

"Release," she said.

She took off her glasses and her gray-green eyes twinkled in the sunlight. She smiled a strange smile.

"You're under arrest," said Sadie.

FBI and local police were all over the street and the church. Jeff ran up the driveway, glaring at Sadie and shaking his head.

Sadie looked back at the man and leaned over his dog-bitten and bleeding body.

"Tell your boss not to send two men to do one women's job," she whispered.

THE MAGNETIC DOOR

═══════════

Sadie sat on the couch, her long dark-brown hair tied back and her gray-green eyes teary. She stroked Nigel's velvet brown and black fur, letting out a deep sigh of irritation. It had been a failed ending to a struggle with her boss, Special Agent White. He had informed her that the narcotic task force now included another person. FBI Agent Sadie Barker and her dog Nigel had collaborated alone for years. That's the way she preferred it. Sadie had gotten used to her undercover persona, a blind person and Nigel her guide dog. Now she had to pretend to be married. This made Sadie furious. She agreed because she wanted to work this case. There had been several deaths of minors in the community. So, she agreed to share the case with Anderson.

Anderson Cobb was a tall burly guy with dark brown eyes the color of hot chocolate. In another environment, Sadie might have even considered him attractive. Sadie didn't let herself think like that. Everyone knew she was all business. Nigel had warmed up to Anderson the first time they met. In Sadie's eyes, he couldn't be all-bad if Nigel liked him.

The condo complex was in a middle-class neighborhood. There had been several drug overdoses and arrests. The drug task force hadn't gotten the kingpin or figured out how the illegal drugs were distributed. That's why they needed Sadie and Nigel to discover what was out-of-the-ordinary. If they pretended to be married, the task force thought Sadie and Anderson could get familiar with the neighbors and determine if they could flush out the dope traffickers.

The government, under a fictitious corporation, owned their second-floor condo. They had assigned different agents to use it. It wasn't unusual for this area. There were many government contractors operating in and out of it because of the defense plant. The condo had a view of the entrances and yards. They had set the surveillance equipment up for Sadie and Anderson. There were constant cameras videotaping the people in the complex and their visitors.

Sadie and Nigel had new updated equipment. Her cover was still that they considered her legally blind, but could see shadows. Her new glasses contained an updated camera, updated computer and updated cell phone with voice commands. Nigel's service vest had state-of-the-art technology equipment along with a pistol. Anderson's cover was that he worked at home as a computer programmer. Sadie started her routine of walking around the neighborhood and filming as she wandered. She was looking for anything out-of-the-ordinary. Most of the people who lived in the complex worked in the daytime. Some worked from home. Others worked second or third shift at the defense plant a few streets over. None of these people seemed to fit a drug trafficker's profile.

Esther, the condo queen, knew everything about everyone in the complex and was more than eager to share it with Sadie.

Whenever Sadie and Nigel took a stroll, they ran into Esther. She had questions for them, as if to trick them into revealing a forgotten secret. Sadie thought this was questionable behavior. Or maybe she was just snooping. Esther was in her mid-forties, but she looked like she was in her late fifties. The skin on her face discolored from years of smoking, and she had developed premature facial wrinkles. She was slim, with bleach-blonde hair, and there was no mistaking the smell of cigarettes whenever she was around. She was constantly picking up around the condo. That too was odd, since there was a maintenance person who came several times a week. Sadie spoke with Anderson about it and even though he thought she was an unlikely suspect, he said he would have a background check run on her.

Sadie and Nigel walked at different times to meet and film the people who lived in the complex. At night, Sadie and Anderson went over her walk footage and the apartments cameras looking for something they could use.

Anderson, Sadie, and Nigel kept this routine over several weeks and then spotted something odd. The maintenance for the complex came with four bags of garbage and put them in the dumpster every other week. That's when Sadie suggested a dumpster dive.

"I'll do it," said Anderson.

Sadie agreed. The last thing she wanted to do was climb into a dumpster again. She had done that before on other assignments. There was always foul-smelling garbage, ants, and other critters in there. They waited until early morning. Sadie and Nigel would be the lookout. If anyone came, she would claim she couldn't sleep. As Sadie was chatting with Anderson while he crawled around in the dumpster, a neighbor came around the corner. Nigel barked.

"What are you doing out here?" a huge bearded man asked.

"I couldn't sleep," Sadie said. "Why are you out this late?" She could see the garbage bag in his hand.

"Emptying my garbage. I work the second shift," he said. "You must be the blind girl."

They both laughed.

"The white cane and the dog gave you away," he quipped. "Let me introduce myself. I'm Casey from building two, apartment three. I work at the plant. Are you always walking around this late at night?" he asked.

"Sometimes," said Sadie. "Have you ever heard of Circadian rhythm sleep disorder?"

"Yes, I was a medic in the military," Casey answered.

Anderson was trying to stay still in the dumpster, but he was being bitten and stung by his new buddies, hungry ants. They were crawling all over him.

Anderson spoke to Sadie's earpiece. "Get rid of him. I need to get out."

Sadie smiled to herself and asked Casey a few more questions.

"Damn it, Sadie, I mean it. I'm being chewed by these vicious ants," he said with irritation in his voice.

Sadie excused herself and walked away. Casey did the same. When Casey went into his building, Sadie doubled back to help Anderson out of the dumpster. He was climbing out, covered in trash with odors of foul mixtures of things. He stormed passed Sadie and Nigel. His calm, friendly, and pleasant demeanor was diminishing. He was fuming and murmuring something under his breath. Sadie just stood there and didn't say a word. Had she gone too far?

When Sadie returned to the condo, the pungent smell of garbage permeated the air. The shower was on, and Anderson's clothes were in a bag on the floor.

Sadie called out to him, "Are you up-to-date with your rabies shots?"

The shower stopped, and Anderson appeared in the kitchen.

"Hilarious, Sadie. You're enjoying this too much," he snapped. "Next time, you can go."

The noise of an automobile pulling into the complex and the intense lights that lit up their living room wall startled them. Two dark figures got out of a car and made their way to the dumpster. One of them lay on the ground and crawled underneath the orange dumpster with several small bags. Then he crawled back out with one larger bag. They got back into the car and drove off.

Sadie and Anderson looked at each other.

"Not in the dumpster but underneath," snapped Anderson.

Sadie could tell it still disturbed him about the dumpster dive and Casey.

"Let's go back and see what we can find," said Sadie.

"No!" said Anderson. "I have had enough trash for one night." He turned and went to bed.

Sadie looked at Nigel and petted his silky fur. "I think he's pissed at me," she thought. He was right. Tomorrow would be better.

When Anderson came into the living room sleepy eyed and tired, Sadie was fast at work. "Working with her is amazing," thought Anderson. She had more energy than anyone he'd ever met. Nigel wagged his tail and Anderson petted him.

"Look," he started. "I'm sorry I got so upset last night. You know damn well you were enjoying me being in that dumpster being bitten just a little too much."

Sadie shook her head. "I'm sorry. You're right," she answered.

"So, what have you figured out while the entire world was sleeping?" he questioned.

Sadie pointed to one of the computer screens. There was the maintenance man, Rusty. He put his own garbage bags in every other week. He would do repair work during that time and turn the condo cameras in another direction. Why? That was a question they knew they both had to answer. They went to work on how they would figure out what was under that dumpster.

The three of them went for a walk in the morning, inspecting the outside of the dumpster to see if there was anything obvious. There wasn't. As they were talking to each other, Esther appeared with a dark-skinned man in his late twenties. She introduced him as her grandson. It surprised Sadie. She had never seen anyone with Esther before. Esther never said she had children. Sadie decided when they got back to the condo that she would see where Esther's background investigation was.

"He'll be staying with me for a few months. Just wanted you and the dog to be at ease with him."

Anderson put out his hand to shake the young man's hand. "Nice to meet you," he said.

The couple and their dog walked away. They realized they had to get under the dumpster and see what the two dark figures had been doing the night before. Anderson thought to himself, "Sadie was right. We should have gone right after the two characters left. I shouldn't have let my personal feelings get in the way."

"I think I've figured this out," said Sadie. "We can put a camera on Nigel's back and he can crawl around underneath the dumpster and record it. Then maybe we can figure out what is under there. Keep everyone away from the dumpster for at least fifteen minutes."

The three of them made their way to the orange monster once more in the early morning. Sadie gave Nigel the command and under the dumpster he went, crossing from one end to the next.

He videoed the complete bottom of the dumpster. Anderson was maintaining a lookout for anyone who appeared. Nigel came out from the dumpster as Casey came around the corner. Sadie grabbed Nigel's harness. She signaled Anderson to stay in the dark.

"Walking your dog again?" Casey asked.

She hesitated for a moment and then replied, "Listen, I told you before I live in darkness. I don't care if it's day or night. When the dog has to go, he has to go," she said.

"How did you recognize that I'm the same guy from last night?" he questioned. "Maybe you're not blind." He lurched at her. Nigel went into attack mode. He stuck his large ninety-five-pound muscular body between them. Casey stepped back, flung his garbage into the trash bin, and stormed off.

Anderson came out of his hiding place.

"What hell was that all about?" he asked.

"Dammed if I know," replied Sadie. "Let's look at this video-tape and see what's under this dumpster."

They returned to the condo and ran the video from Nigel's vest. There was a narrow, hidden handle on the dumpster bottom. It was most likely magnetic. This must be the hiding place. But who was their mark?

"Let's go open the door," said Anderson. "The worst we can do is piss off someone because we stole their stash. I'll crawl under now that we know how to get in. Make sure you have your safety off your gun. This could get dangerous."

"Okay," replied Sadie.

The three of them were rounding the corner when they spotted two dark figures at the dumpster. One dropped and slid underneath the dumpster. The other was the lookout.

Sadie signaled Nigel and Anderson. It was time for action. They waited until the image slipped out from underneath the trash receptacle, stood, and started walking away.

"Stop! FBI," said Sadie.

Anderson placed his flashlight on them. They dropped the bags and ran. Nigel sprang into action, getting one to the ground. His pearly razor teeth tore in their flesh, scarlet welling up in the wounds. Sadie tackled the other, rolling around in the grass several times. Anderson grabbed the character off of her and got him handcuffed and to his feet. Sadie gave Nigel a command to release, and Anderson cuffed the other person. He yanked off both of their black masks.

Sadie and Anderson just stared at them. It was Esther and Casey.

"You bitch. I knew you weren't blind. I wanted to bury you since you came here," she said with a seething in her voice.

"Shut up, Esther," snapped Casey.

Sadie pulled out her glasses, her gray-green eyes sparkling in the night-light. She grinned a peculiar grin. It was a smile of approval of what they had accomplished.

"Always go with your gut. You're both are under arrest," replied Sadie.

THE ENDOWMENT OF JEREMIAH STONE

"Damn you, George Warren, for getting into an intense argument with me," thought Isabella. Detective Isabella Stone was disturbed by what transpired at the dedication ceremony at her great-great-grandfather's library.

Sophia, her twin sister, was right to step into the middle of the disagreement. Even though they were twins, they were different in looks, personalities, and especially in their tempers. Isabella had long blonde hair, blue eyes, and a tall, slim body. Sophia had dark hair, brown eyes, and a slightly heftier frame. Isabella was talkative and outgoing, while Sophia was quiet and kept to herself.

Isabella sipped her wine on the deck and gazed at the sparkling blue water. The sunset filled the sky with orange, yellow, and red colors. It overpowered the blue sky and reflected in the water, as it crept lower and lower. The pleasant breeze, the sweet smell of the salty water, the sound of waves crashing against each other, all completed the scene of a perfect sunset.

Isabella inherited this house on the water in Smithville, Maine from her great-grandfather. She loved it as a child, and when he died, he bequeathed it to her. It was the finest gift he could have given her.

Her cell phone rang, transporting her back to reality. It was Sophia. What did she want? They just parted a few hours ago.

"Hi, Sophia. I am not apologizing to George Warren?" Isabella said.

"I know," she responded. "You can't. He passed away."

"What?" said Isabella.

Just then, two homicide detectives from her squadron were coming on to her deck.

"I'll call you back, Sophia," said Isabella.

Lieutenant Parker, her supervisor, appeared first, then Sergeant Mason.

Steadying her nerves, Isabella asked, "Out for a Sunday stroll, gentlemen?"

"That's what I admire about you, Stone. You're always joking," said Parker. "We'd like to talk to you about the library dedication."

Lieutenant Parker didn't care for Isabella. He knew that she came from old money, and she was the first and only female detective in their unit. His wrinkled face hung like an old leather jacket. He didn't age gracefully, and his large-rimmed and thick-lensed glasses hid most of his face. Any time he could give Isabella a hard time, he did, and he pointed out her mistakes.

Isabella and Sophia came from a prominent family in the town. They went to private schools and Ivy League colleges. Their parents hoped they would enter the family's law firm after college, but neither woman wanted that life. Isabella chose police work. Sophia became a librarian. Both women did a lot of community service and represented their family at many events like the one they attended this weekend for their great-great-grandfather.

"Isabella," said Lieutenant Parker. "I understand that George Warren, the trustee of Jeremiah Stone's endowment, and you had words at the dedication."

"Words? No. More like a discussion," retorted Isabella. "I wanted to know how the endowment money ceased to exist for seventy-five years. Then it was found, and they built a library in my great-great-grandfather's name. I think that's great detective work," snickered Isabella.

"From what we understand," interrupted Sergeant Mason, "you made a scene, and Sophia had to step in."

"That's not true!" snapped Isabella.

"Quote: 'I'll take care of him.' Now he's dead. Did you say that, Isabella?" asked Mason.

"I may have whispered something like that. But do you think I meant it?" replied Isabella, annoyed.

Sergeant Mason didn't respond. He just glared at her with his gray piercing eyes and dark, greasy slicked-back hair.

"Ask Sophia if you don't believe me. We spent the whole time together."

"Trust me, we will," replied Lieutenant Parker.

"How did George die?" asked Isabella.

"We must wait for the medical examiner's report," said Parker. "You'll be on desk duty until we solve the case. You can't see any of the evidence. Understand?"

"What?" said Isabella. "You can't think I had anything to do with his death. What would I have to gain from it?"

"Don't know," the detectives replied.

"Remember, desk duty. And don't stick your nose where it doesn't belong," the Lieutenant said.

Parker and Mason turned and went down the staircase to their unmarked car. In the dark, they couldn't see Sophia parked across the street, waiting for them to leave. She watched them leave, then pulled into the driveway, and bolted out of her car. She rushed up the long staircase. The noise startled Isabella. When she turned, her blue eyes couldn't believe it was Sophia.

"What are you doing here?" she asked.

"Are you crazy? A man is dead. A man you threatened to take care of. Or did you forget that?" said Sophia, gasping for air from running up a flight of stairs. "Did you have your weapons with you this weekend?" Sophia blurted out.

"No, they're both in my safe. Where they still are," Isabella replied, annoyed by the question. "Sophia, do you think I would ever kill someone? Unless it was in the line of duty? Especially over lost money?"

"I don't know what to think. What about the time you went for a walk? Where did you go? Did you see or talk to anyone?" said Sophia, weeping and trembling, just thinking about what had happened at the library. They had purchased a giant-sized dictionary and dedicated it in their parents' name. For all she knew, someone had struck Mr. Warren with the dictionary and killed him.

"Sophia, calm down," said Isabella. "I strolled on the waterfront, and I didn't see anyone. What did you do while I was gone? You had plenty of time to get over to the library and do one of your flashy black-belt moves on him."

Sophia clenched her fists and sucked air through her teeth, thinking she'd do nothing like that. Yet she had thought Isabella might. What's wrong with them? They couldn't kill anyone. They had good lives and enough money to do anything they wanted to.

"I'm so sorry," said Sophia. She sauntered over and hugged her sister. "I'm drained. I'm going home and get some rest." She turned and walked down the stairs and got into her car. Isabella waved from the deck. Sophia only lived a few streets over from Isabella. She had inherited their parents' home, not on the water, but an old Victorian filled with antiques.

Isabella sat back down and took a big sip of wine. "What a night," she thought. She retreated to her study and took out the papers about the endowment. Then she turned on the lights to the deck and began struggling to piece the events of the evening together. A golden ray appeared in the early morning sky. She watched as it widened into a big ball of fire that heated the earth. It moved across the sky with a grace as if to own it. She had some idea of what happened to the money and where it had been all these years. Even though most of it was circumstantial evidence. She could prove intent, motive, and opportunity. "Time for a shower and strong coffee," Isabella thought.

The first drop of water hit her slender body. The warm droplets formed steam as Isabella stood there without moving. All the information about the endowment rolled around in her head. How much clearer could the facts be? She closed her eyes as the hot steam enveloped her body. As she washed the shampoo suds out of her blonde hair, the water sent a stream down her back. The coffee aroma wafted up from the kitchen. Drying hastily, she shuffled to the kitchen. She inhaled the strong aroma of coffee. Isabella knew her day would be long.

She dialed her sister's number. Sophia picked up on the first ring.

"Did you stay up all night," Sophia asked.

"I did," Isabella laughed. "I think I have discovered some clues in some journals." Their great-great-grandfather had left detailed information about the endowment. Isabella thought she had discovered a reason to commit a murder. The two of them would have to work together to collect the evidence since Isabella was on desk duty. They both couldn't believe the suspect. Isabella explained to Sophia what she had to do and how to do it and then got dressed.

Isabella's instructions were precise as always. When they played as kids, Isabella had to be the boss. Sophia's first stop was the family's law firm. The sisters had no legal interest in the firm, but they still used their services and maintained stock shares. Sophia looked up all the information: why the endowment started and who the administrators were. She then called Isabella's cell phone.

"I have the information. And you're right."

"Great," said Isabella. "Now, if we could only find out how George died, we will have enough evidence to prove who the murderer is."

"I might be able to get that information," replied Sophia.

"How?" questioned Isabella.

"Remember Sidney?" asked Sophia.

"Yes," answered Isabella.

"He works in the medical examiner's office, and he asked me for a date," Sophia chuckled.

"Who's the detective here?" joked Isabella.

"I'll call you back," said Sophia.

Ten minutes later, Sophia called Isabella with the information Sidney had given her. She also had a dinner date next week. A small price to pay for the information he had provided. The two women now had pieced the crime together.

Isabella went down to the evidence locker to see if they had tagged the weapon that killed Mason. It appeared from the report that it had not been found yet. Did the killer take it with him? She had to find out.

"Stone, what are you doing down here?" an intense voice asked. It was Parker.

"Just looking through some old case files since I have desk duty," she answered.

"Good. That's what you should do," he said.

"Don't threaten me," snapped Isabella as she walked up the stairs.

That evening, Isabella drove to the library and crawled under the crime scene tape. Dressed in black, she hurried through the dimly lit library. The dictionary was still on the stand where it had been at the ceremony. She looked around to see if the weapon had fallen under anything. "They must have searched this area when they discovered the body," she thought. Not finding the weapon, she started to sneak out the same way she came in. Suddenly, she heard footsteps coming her way. She slipped behind a bookcase and sucked her whole body into it. The person walked around for a while, searching the same places Isabella had searched. The intruder gave up and left. She waited for several minutes before making her way out. She had been smart enough to park several streets over.

As she started her car, there was a tap on the window, scaring her to death. Trapped in her car, she grabbed her weapon. Another tap. Slowly Isabella lowered the window. It was Sergeant Mason.

"Are you following me?" asked Isabella.

"I saw you walking out of the crime scene. Looking for the weapon you left behind?" Mason asked.

"What weapon? I don't even know how George died. So, what would I be focusing on? Anyway, I'm on desk duty, or did you forget?"

Mason laughed. "That means nothing to you. Parker thinks you did it, and he is collecting anything he can to prove it. This is your first and last warning. Don't get involved. Just do as you're told." Mason turned and walked away with his arms swinging back and forth and his stilt-like legs carried him into the dark.

Isabella let out a deep sigh, her heart racing. Was he the murderer? She started her car and started driving home. Sophia called. She told her what happened with Mason.

"There is more to this story than just an endowment," said Sophia. "Parker or Mason wants you to be the primary suspect for this crime. Do you think you can get them to the library tomorrow?"

"Why?" asked Isabella.

After looking over the files again from the law firm, Sophia realized there was spreadsheets in a section of the library about the endowment. They were put there because no one would ever look there.

"Okay, I'll set it up and call you," said Isabella.

When Isabella arrived at the station in the morning, she marched into Parker's office. Passing Mason on the way, she gestured him to follow her.

"We need to go to the crime scene. Sophia has found some new evidence she wants to show us."

Parker raised an eyebrow, anxious about what Isabella had just asked him. "Don't forget you're on desk duty, not this case." But his curiosity was heightened, and he wondered what the two women had found. Isabella, Mason, and Parker drove together to the library. Isabella called Sophia to meet them.

Meeting outside the library, they walked in silence to the scene.

"You'd better not be up to any funny business?" said Parker.

Any other day, people would fill this library by reading, doing research, and appreciating the tranquility the library provides. Parker cut the tape as they wandered in.

Sophia pulled out some ledgers from a cupboard hidden in the library's corner. She produced the spreadsheets that proved someone had been stealing the interest on the endowment for years. That person was the father of the victim, George Warren. Before that, Lieutenant Parker's grandfather handled the funding. Both men had worked for Jeremiah Stone. There had been rumors for years that Mr. Stone had an illegitimate son and had never acknowledged or supported him. That person was Lieutenant Parker's grandfather.

"Old man Stone owed my family that money. My God, the way my grandfather grew up and the way my family was so poor. You two had it handed to you," said Parker, adjusting his thick-rimmed glasses.

Sophia realized that if that was true, they were related to Lieutenant Parker. Maybe an uncle? She went to say something, but Parker drew his gun and ordered them all to step back. As they did, Isabella knocked over the large dictionary. As the dictionary tumbled off the sizeable wooden pedestal, it opened and from the spine of the book came a bloody letter opener. The commotion of the letter opener and the book hitting the floor startled everyone, giving Isabella and Mason time to draw their weapons.

"Put the weapon down," said Isabella.

"Come on, Parker, you don't want to out this way," Mason said.

"You two are fast," said Parker.

He raised his hand and pointed his revolver at Isabella and cocked and fired. The sound shook the walls of the library. The intensity from Isabella's and Sergeant Mason's weapons echoed in their ears.

Parker looked right them, stumbled, and landed on the dictionary. The bloody letter opener was next to his body.

Mason ran to him. He put his fingertips to his neck to feel for a pulse. Mason shook his head. Parker was gone.

Their family skeletons would no longer lurk in the closet.

The secret of who Parker really was, and the endowment, died with him.

THE MIRROR IMAGE

The magical and spiritual light sent a small beacon bouncing off the stained-glass windows of the stone church. Changing light floated across the floor, inviting Katherine to let her herself become distracted. Air vibrating from the pipe organ filled the church with various musical harmonies. The black-robed choir sang "Amazing Grace." Small, tiny crystal beads crept out of Katherine's eyes, one after another. They rolled down her face. Her father put his arm around her and squeezed her tight.

"It will be all right," he said.

The minister was talking about her grandfather, but she couldn't hear the words. All she recalled was the last time she was here for a memorial service. It was her mother's and grandmother's. Katherine was 14 years old. They were killed in a fatal automobile accident. Now, 15 years later, she was here for her grandfather's memorial service. "Will my father be next?" she wondered.

A blank, emotionless expression swept over her face as the realization of the moment gradually seeped in. Paralyzed by the immediate perception of isolation, she closed her eyes and gazed into the fields of nothingness. Katherine felt the water creep out of her eyes and she whispered softly to herself, "This too shall pass."

Her mind strayed back to the two women's service and how sad her father and grandfather had been. Both wept openly in church. She always felt that they never had gotten over their spouses' deaths and had put all their love into her. Both of them were her rock and had seen her through all of her tough times. Now the rock split in half.

Katherine turned to her father and forced a smile. "I'll miss him," she whispered.

"Me too," he said.

Katherine Harper had taken care of her grandfather when he had become ill. The doctors didn't know what made him so sick, so they ran all kinds of tests. He would go in and out of consciousness and kept muttering, "I should have told the secret."

Katherine tried to get him to tell her what he meant, but he would just look at her with tear-filled eyes. When she told her father about it, he assured her he was just delusional. She was sure that he was right, but she felt the need to investigate. How would she do that? She didn't even know what she was searching for. "I'll call Isabella," she thought.

Detective Isabella Stone was her roommate in law school, and they had been friends for years. If anyone could help her, it was Isabella.

After the receiving line at the service, there was a sit-down dinner for several hundred people. She and her father were glad when it was over. They drove in silence back to her grandfather's home, which would become Katherine's. Her grandmother and grandfather always told her when she was a little girl that it would be hers someday. Her father owned his own home, which was as exquisite as her grandfather's.

"Do you want me to stay with you tonight?" asked her father.

"No, I'll be fine," said Katherine.

"You seem so preoccupied," said her father.

"I can't get grandfather's ramblings out of my head. What do you think the secret is?" asked Katherine.

"He was sick, and his mind was playing tricks on him," snapped her father.

Katherine felt her father didn't want to discuss her grandfather's last days. It was like he knew what the secret was, but didn't want her to know. "That's foolish," she thought. "My father would never do that." They didn't have any secrets from each other.

Katherine tried to change the mood in the room. "Tomorrow I'm going to go up and start clearing out the attic. What do you think?" she said.

Her father chuckled. "Good luck. That place hasn't been cleaned in years. So, if I can't find you, I will look up there and see you fell into something," he laughed.

"Hilarious, dad. You're always a comedian," laughed Katherine.

Her father rose and kissed her goodnight and left.

Katherine just sat there and tears flowed down her checks. She would miss her grandfather. When she graduated from law school, he had hired her to work in his accounting firm's law division. Now her father and she were partners of the company. She headed up the law department.

The next morning, Katherine unlocked the door and walked up the stairs to the attic. She felt unsettled. Something was troubling her and she didn't know what it was.

It was the stairs! There were footprints in the dust. Her father had said that no one had been up there for years. When she was a little girl, she was never allowed to go up there. The door was always locked. The stairs creaked and groaned. She felt a cold rush of air wash over her, so cold it made the hair on the back of her neck stand up. She couldn't turn back. She was drawn to whatever presence resided in the attic's iciness.

The sunlight beamed down on the dusty panes of the glass windows, illuminating the room ever so slightly. She felt frightened, but her sense of adventure made her investigate the attic a little more. There was something magical about this room that drew her in. All that antique furniture, the piles of boxes, and just junk. Yet there was something sinister about this room. The air was icy cold and even though she was the only living soul in the room, there was a feeling that something else was watching her every move. As if its eyes were burning down on her back like the heat of the sun. The darkness of this terrible thing was something evil.

There was dusty old junk everywhere. It was hard for Katherine to move. She coughed and sneezed and the dampness smelled like mildew. "Next time I come up here, I'll wear a mask," she thought. After about an hour, she spotted two leather boxes that would change her life.

She opened one and spotted old medals from a society in Ohio and a stack of various stock certificates. The other one contained letters addressed to a P.O. box under her grandfather's name. But most surprising were the pictures of her grandfather with people she didn't recognize, but looked familiar. She gathered up both boxes and went downstairs. When she approached the bottom, her father was standing there grinning.

"You thought I was joking," he said.

"I did," laughed Katherine.

"You look like a chimney sweep," laughed her father.

"Look at all my treasures," she burst out like a small child.

"You found something?" questioned her father.

"Lots of old stock certificates, some medals, a box of letters, and pictures," she answered.

The look on her father's face told the full story. He looked amazed and angry at the same time. He made Katherine feel like she had felt as a child when he didn't approve of something she had done. He didn't have to say anything. His eyes and his facial expressions said it all. Katherine walked into the kitchen and found a cloth to wipe off the boxes and then went into the living room where her father was sitting. She knew he was angry. She handed him the two boxes. "I'm going to take a shower. Why don't you have a look?" she said.

When she returned, her father was sitting at the dining room table going through the letters and pictures.

"What do you think this means?" asked Katherine.

"I don't know," replied her father with a quiver in his voice. "I do know that we need to check out the stock certificates. If they're authentic, you could be a millionaire many times over."

"What about the letters and pictures?" questioned Katherine.

"I don't know what to think. Is my whole life a lie?" said her father. As he said that he broke down and wept. Katherine comforted him.

"Dad, let's just figure out what this means," she said.

"How do you plan to do that?" he said with a deep irritation in his voice.

"I have an idea. How about Isabella?" Katherine asked.

"Isabella Stone!" her father said with a raised voice.

"Yes, she has the means to look these things up. Being a detective has perks," said Katherine.

"I forbid you from doing that," yelled her father.

She had never seen her father so angry. But she wasn't a child, and she wanted to know who these people in the pictures were.

Why did her grandfather belong to some society in Ohio? Why did he just put all those stock certificates in a box and forget about them?

"No," she shouted. "I'm not a child and I won't be treated like one," she said.

"I don't and I won't have any part of this," her father said.

He got up and stalked out the house, slamming the door.

Katherine grabbed her cell phone and dialed Isabella's number.

"Homicide. Detective Stone," said the voice on the other end.

"Hi. It's me, Katherine."

"Kate, how are you?" said Isabella.

"Can you come over to the house this evening? I have a problem and I need your help," asked Katherine.

"Sure. How is seven?" answered Isabella.

"Great. I'll prepare dinner," she replied.

Isabella arrived at seven o'clock and Katherine greeted her. They had dinner and she told Isabella what she had found. Isabella sat there in complete shock. She knew Katherine's grandfather and couldn't believe it.

"There has to be an answer for all of this," said Isabella.

She took down all the information and told Katherine she would see what she could uncover. She promised to get back to her soon.

Katherine went to bed that night convinced she would find out what the family secret was.

Her father came over the next morning. There were black circles under his eyes. He was totally beside himself.

"Dad, did you get any sleep?" asked Katherine.

"Not much. I'm so confused. I know there is an answer for all of this. I wish you didn't find out any of these things. Our lives have been altered by this," he sobbed.

Katherine told him about her call to Isabella and how she was going to look into this. Her father wasn't sure he wanted to find out anything else.

"We have to," said Katherine. "Our lives could be a complete lie. I want to know who my family actually is."

It took Isabella several days and many calls to the FBI to track down the Harper family in Ohio. Unfortunately, there was only one person alive, Rosemary Harper.

The phone rang just as Katherine was deciding if she wanted to take another look in the attic.

"Hello, this is Katherine."

"Hi, it's Isabella. I have something to show you. Can I come over?"

"Sure. Can I invite my dad?" asked Katherine.

"I think it is best if you and I look at the information first. Then you can show him," replied Isabella.

"Okay," said Katherine. "See you soon."

Isabella arrived shortly after the phone conversation. She put all the information on the dining room table. There were some pictures of the same family with another young man. If they were related, it would be Katherine's aunt, uncle, and cousin. Or so Isabella thought. There was a wedding picture of her grandfather with his other wife. Also, there were two accident reports. Her grandfather had been reported killed on a mountain climb expedition, but his body was never recovered. The other was an automobile accident that took the lives of three of the Harper family. This was getting too coincidental. Katherine cried as she did her father walked in.

"What's the matter?" he asked

Isabella showed him what she had showed Katherine. It was so incredible that his father could have gotten away with this for so long. He was a fraud, not and honorable man like people thought. He adored his wife and cherished his son, so he let people believe. He had traveled for many years as an insurance man until he opened his accounting firm. He was a bigamist. Katherine's father couldn't deal with anything else.

"Dad," Katherine said. "Let's get all the evidence before we come to any conclusion. I don't know what this is all about, but I'm going to Ohio to find out."

"I'll go with you," replied her father.

"No, I'm going with Isabella," answered Katherine.

"Katherine, this is family business. I want to leave it that way," replied her father. "Isabella can air her family's dirty laundry in the papers and on the news, but we aren't going to do that."

Isabella was stunned by Greg's outburst, but elected not to say anything. Katherine was embarrassed by her father's nasty words. She too decided not to say anything because she didn't want to have a fight. Her father was acting so strange and he seemed angry all the time. She didn't like this side of him.

"Isabella has made all the reservations and has gotten all the information we need to contact Rosemary. We are leaving in the morning for the airport. I will let you know what we find out. You need to go home and rest," Katherine said.

"I know I can't stop you, but remember you've brought this all on our family," said her father in a chilling voice.

Katherine couldn't get the words out of her head. His words were threatening and frightening. This wasn't the father she knew. But, was anyone in this family?

The two women went through security at the airport in private because of Isabella's weapon and police status. They got their rental car and accompanied two detectives from the Ohio police force to the station. They were shown the files on the

Harper family. Mainly the same reports as the had previously seen. This whole thing was getting stranger and stranger by the moment. When they were done at the police station, they drove to 22 Laurel Street, where Rosemary lived.

As they drove up the driveway, they both had a look of sheer surprise on their face. The house was a mirror image of Katherine's grandfather's home in Maine. It needed repair, but other than that they were the same. The front door opened and a young, slender redheaded woman stepped onto the porch. She could have been Katherine's twin. There couldn't be any doubt that they were related.

"Can I help you?" she asked.

Isabella opened the car door and stepped out and flashed her badge. "We are looking for Rosemary Harper," she answered.

"That's me," she replied.

Katherine stepped out of the car. The look on Rosemary's face was complete surprise.

"Do I know you?" asked Rosemary.

"I think we are related," answered Katherine.

"That's not possible. We are the only Harpers. I'm an only child and everyone else is gone," said Rosemary.

"I am also an only child," replied Katherine. "I found pictures in my grandfather's attic after his death. They are pictures of your family. I think my grandfather faked his death here in Ohio so he could open an accounting firm in Maine."

"I find that hard to believe," said Rosemary. "My grandfather was such a loving man. He left us with sufficient wealth. I don't know what to say. Let's go inside."

When they entered the house, it took Katherine and Isabella's breath away. It was a mirror image of the other house. Rosemary sensed their uneasiness and wondered to herself if maybe she shouldn't have asked them in. "What's wrong?" Rosemary asked.

"The house is completely the same on the outside and inside. It's like a mirror image of where I live," answered Katherine.

Rosemary served several pots of coffee and they talked until late into the night. Isabella took several pages of notes. She planned to return to the police station in the morning to do some more work and then pick up Katherine from the house. Katherine planned to return in the morning to have some private time with Rosemary.

The next morning, Katherine took a taxi to the house. When she knocked on the door no one answered. She tried the handle and it opened. Katherine could hear loud voices coming from the living room. One of them sounded like her father. She walked down the hallway quietly so she wouldn't be heard. She could hear her father yelling at someone. She stepped into the room. It was Rosemary. She was sobbing.

"Dad, what are you doing here?" Katherine said with a harsh tone.

He turned to look at Katherine with piercing eyes. They were red, like flame, and they seemed to look right through her.

"I'm here to settle this problem once and for all." His voice seemed that of a stranger. "She has to be dealt with, just like the others."

"Others?" screamed Katherine. "What others?"

"All our family and hers," said her father.

"Have you lost your mind?" yelled Katherine.

As she said those words, a gun appeared in her father's hand. He laughed, a haunting laugh. The two women tried to move closer. He cocked the gun. "Don't," he said.

He pulled the trigger.

Katherine pushed Rosemary aside. The round ripped through Katherine like a piece of hot steel. Another shot rang out. The noise vibrated off the walls. Her father fell next to Katherine's limp body. Isabella had come to pick Katherine up. She could hear the yelling as she entered the house, but she couldn't get down to the room in time to stop the first shot. She and Rosemary ran to Katherine. She was gone, as was her father. Isabella looked at Rosemary. She was weeping.

"The family secret is now yours," Isabella said.

THE STAINED GLASS WINDOW

Gabriella Bowman considered herself a modern-day treasure hunter. There wasn't a flea market, thrift store, or consignment shop that Gabby didn't know about or hadn't visited. On this day, she spotted a charming but neglected piece of stained glass. That was her favorite thing to find. With some white vinegar and olive oil, it would be as good as new. What fascinated her was that the piece had a business card attached to it. On the back of the business card, there was a phone number and address. Salisbury Cove, Maine. A place she had spent many vacations as a child with her sister. The cost was fourteen dollars.

Gabby was surprised when the cashier said, "That'll be seven dollars because all wooden framed items are half price today." Gabby was thrilled. She loved a bargain.

She went home and cleaned the piece. It was impressive and looked terrific in her hallway window. The stained glass glistened in the light, but there was a section that was discolored. It looked like it had been broken and then repaired. She remembered the business card she had removed and placed on the counter when she cleaned the piece. There was the name of a Glass Company, an address, and a phone number. No email address. "Before their time," she thought. She went on her computer and looked up the company. It closed years ago, but another company took its place. She turned the business card over and looked at the address and phone number. No name. Gabby looked up the phone number, and to her amazement she discovered the owner was a former state senator and college administrator from Maine. Senator Lance Grayson, who had succumbed to a heart attack at his home. His long-time assistant Edith Baxter had found him.

Gabby was familiar with this area of Maine because of her summers there. She would contacted her sister, who lived in New Hampshire, to see if she would like to solve another mystery. How had the stained-glass piece ended up in a thrift shop in Connecticut?

Gabby called her. "Are you up for another mystery?" she asked.

"Sure," she laughed.

Her sister, Jacqueline Edwards, was excited about another treasure hunt and another mystery. Since they were young girls, they regularly played sleuths. They now belonged to a group called The Blind Justice Society. Whenever Jacqueline visited Gabby, they met at Harriett's Tavern. They were retired and the had time to go off. Jacquelin, the oldest, had moved to New Hampshire to start her teaching career in science. She was a thin, gray-haired woman, with faint streaks of red that were once her hair color and sparkling baby-blue eyes. Gabby taught History and she loved making it come alive for her students. She had short golden-blond hair and a similar build as Jacqueline. She had the same sparkling baby-blue eyes. There wasn't a doubt in the world that these women were sisters.

Gabby packed her suitcase and set out for the drive from Connecticut to New Hampshire. It was about a three-and-a-half-hour drive to Jacqueline's. She was waiting for her in the driveway.

"Come on in and tell me what we will be doing," Jacqueline said.

The two women chatted for hours and planned what they would do the next day when they got to Maine. The first thing was to go to the glass company and chat with the proprietors. They arrived at Midtown Glass Company around ten. It was a charming place with unique pieces of colored glass, and there was a repair section. They went there.

Gabby spoke with a tall, brown-haired, bearded man behind the counter about what she had found. He told them that there were some files downstairs about the old company in the basement.

"You're welcome to look through them," he offered.

It thrilled the women as they climbed down the old wooden stairs into the dark, dungeon-like basement. The files were in order by job number. They removed the cards. The piece belonged to Senator Grayson, and it was broken and brought in for repair. Gabby looked at her sister. "We need to find out when the Senator died. This piece may have something to do with his death," said Gabby.

Jacqueline just shook her head and rolled her baby-blue eyes. She knew better than to say anything.

"We need to look up his death certificate," said Gabby.

Gabby took pictures of the repair slip, and they climbed back up the stairs. They thanked the owner for his help and got back into the car. They put the town hall into the GPS, and off they went.

Jacqueline laughed. "Remember when we were kids and played detective?"

"Yes," said Gabby. "We solved a lot of cases." They both laughed.

The sisters arrived at the town hall quickly. It was a small town. They went inside to talk with the town clerk. The clerk was curious about what their interest was in the senator's death.

"He died of a heart attack," said the clerk.

Gabby told her about the piece of stained glass and the business card attached to it. The clerk's face turned as white as winter snow. Gabby noticed the nametag around the clerk's neck, Edith Baxter. She was Senator Grayson's former personal assistant. Edith was short and stocky, almost fat. Her hair was a mousey-brown and thinning, and she was simply dressed. Gabby decided to just tell her why they were asking questions. After all, it wasn't like she had stolen the piece.

"Ms. Baxter, my sister and I just wondered how the piece ended up in Connecticut," said Gabby.

Edith turned around and hustled into the back room. She returned with the death certificate. Gabby paid her, and the two women looked at it. The date was close to the repair time.

"If you'd like to look at his house, it's for sale on North Road, just out of town. It's been unoccupied since his death. No one seems to want a house someone died in," Edith said.

"How would we get in," asked Gabby.

"There is a key under the doormat," she replied. Edith gave them directions.

The two women thanked her and drove to the house. The house was set far off the road. It had large black iron gates that had long-since been broken. The grass was high, but there was a man-made path to the house. The house had held up nicely for being empty for several years. They opened the door, and to their surprise all the furniture was covered and the interior was in good condition.

"I guess someone keeps this house up," said Gabby.

Jacqueline agreed.

They walked through all the rooms of the house to get a sense of it. The owners had decorated it in soft colors and wooden floors. Gabby tried to figure out where the stained-glass piece may have hung. The chain on the back was short. She had replaced it with a longer one. She noticed a shadow on the wall like the shape of the piece. "That's it," she thought.

"Jacqueline, that's where the piece hung," said Gabby.

"How can you be sure?" Jacqueline asked.

"The shape. It's oval," said Gabby.

She traced the shape with her hand on the wall. Jacqueline could see that she was correct. Gabby crawled around on the floor and moved her hand ever so slowly around.

"What are you doing?" asked Jacqueline.

"Looking for broken glass," she replied.

"If someone used the piece as a weapon, don't you assume they would have cleaned it up?" asked Jacqueline.

Just then, Gabby grabbed her hand. It was bleeding. A piece of small glass stuck out of her hand. Jacqueline tried to help. Gabby stopped her.

"We need to find a broom and clean up," said Gabby.

Suddenly, the front door flung opened, and a large man with gray whiskers and paint-spattered pants stepped inside.

"What are you doing here?" he said in a Maine accent.

The women looked at each other and were silent. He had a rifle in his hand.

"We are interested in purchasing the house," said Gabby.

"Really?" he answered, sounding surprised.

"Yes," they answered together. Their eyes locked on the rifle.

"Somehow I don't believe you," he said in a chilling tone. "I noticed you drive up. My house is next door. I thought you broke into the place. I decided to take a look and bring my best friend." He looked at the rifle. "I'm sorry if I terrified you," he said.

"Let me introduce myself. I'm Garrison Taylor."

Gabby got up from the floor, blood dripping down her arm. She reached inside her pocket and took out a tissue.

"You're bleeding. Let me help," Garrison said.

"It's nothing. I just cut it on a piece of glass," Gabby replied.

"May I ask what you were looking for on the floor?"

"I dropped something and I was trying to find it," she said.

"There have been break-ins. Windows got broken. I thought I cleaned it all up," Garrison replied.

He walked toward Gabby. She put out her hand to stop him.

"I'm fine," she said, pressing the tissue harder on the wound.

"We'll be leaving now," said Jacqueline.

"Sorry if I spooked you both," he said.

"As I told you, there have been break-ins. Things got stolen. One of my sister's pieces was taken. A stained glass she worked on for months. She called it The Sandpiper."

Gabby knew that was the piece she had discovered. It had three sandpiper birds in it. She cleared her throat.

"Who was your sister to Senator Grayson?" asked Gabby.

"Anastasia Taylor, the senator's fiancée," he replied.

"I didn't know he was engaged," replied Gabby.

"They were to get married as soon as he won the senate seat again," he said.

The women looked at each other.

"What happened?"

"Senator Grayson had a secret that his family didn't want everyone to know. He was gay. He tried to hide it because his father threatened to disinherit him. I guessed when he was younger, they said it was a phase he was going through. I think that's why he always had Edith, his assistant, with him," he said.

"His father demanded he find someone and get married. My sister was an up-and-coming artist, and they cared about each other. But he couldn't go through with it, and he broke off the engagement."

"At first, she was resentful. She even said she wanted to kill Grayson. Edith was overjoyed because she was head-over-heels in love with him. You must have met her at the town hall. Not the marrying kind," he laughed.

"Your sister must have known," said Gabby.

"She said there were rumors, but why would you ask someone to marry you just to satisfy your family? Especially when he informed her that he cared for someone else. I guess he couldn't live with that. It's sad, but his death changed everything," he said.

"What happened to your sister?" Gabby asked.

"Anastasia and her husband own the glass company in town," he replied.

Panic set in. Had they spoken to Anastasia's husband? Gabby had shown him a picture of the sandpiper. He knew that they knew it had been repaired. They glanced at each other with fear in their sparkling baby-blue eyes.

"We have to go," Gabby said.

The women turned and walked out the door. Driving out of the driveway, they both talked at once. "Damn it, Gabby, you've mixed us up in something sinister," said Jacqueline.

"I'm sorry. I had no idea," said Gabby.

"We're leaving tomorrow. You should destroy that piece!" shouted Jacqueline.

"Okay. I can't promise I'll destroy the sandpiper, but we will leave," said Gabby.

They drove nonstop to the motel where they were staying. Gabby unlocked the door and turned on the lights. To their surprise someone had ransacked their room. Their luggage had been searched, and someone had flung their clothing all over the place.

Gabby said, "They were looking for the sandpiper. We need to call the police. We aren't safe," she said.

They left the room and went to the motel manager's office and explained what had happened. He hadn't noticed anyone strange hanging around. He called the police, and they arrived quickly.

The first question was, "What did they take?"

"Nothing."

"What were they looking for?"

Gabby couldn't help blurting out, "A stained-glass piece purchased at a thrift store in Connecticut."

The police looked puzzled. "Was it valuable or perhaps a stolen piece?" asked one officer.

Jacqueline held her breath. She knew Gabby would tell them what she suspected.

"I think they used it in the murder of Senator Lance Grayson," replied Gabby.

The officers looked at each other in astonishment.

"Why do you think the senator was murdered," asked the portly officer.

"A gut feeling," said Gabby.

"So, what you're telling me is that you got a stained-glass piece, and now someone in this town wants it back?" the officer questioned.

"Something like that," replied Gabby.

Jacqueline could sense that the officers weren't buying Gabby's theory.

"We called you because someone broke into our room and went through our belongings. We came here to find out how this piece ended up in Connecticut," said Jacqueline.

"Would you two mind coming down to the station and chatting with detective Isabella Stone?" asked the brown-haired officer.

Jacqueline shot Gabby an intense glare. Gabby tried to smile, but she knew her sister was furious with her. Playing detective is one thing, but hinting that there was a murderer loose in this town was another thing.

"We would be glad to," said Gabby.

They all got into the squad car and went to the station. Detective Stone met them at the door and guided them into her office.

"So, you two think someone murdered Senator Grayson?" she asked.

Before Jacqueline could say anything, Gabby said, "Yes."

"May I ask why and how?" she questioned.

"Because his father didn't want the world to know his son was gay," Gabby replied. "I haven't figured out how, but it has something to do with the stained-glass piece."

"Why would you think that?" asked the detective.

"That's the sole thing we have that the murderer would want," Gabby answered.

Detective Stone asked where the piece was. They told her it was in a safe place at Jacqueline's house.

"Could I ask your local police to retrieve it and bring it here?" the detective asked.

Gabby and Jacqueline agreed and told her where the spare key was. It took several hours to get the piece to Maine and a few more days in the lab for testing. It had been repaired and had traces of blood on it. It was a match for the senator's blood. They also found a partial fingerprint. The person wasn't in the system. There was also a high trace of lead.

Gabby and Jacqueline were becoming restless in the safe-house where the police had placed them until all the test results were in. Jacqueline hadn't spoken to Gabby because she was just so angry that she had gotten them into this mess. Jacqueline told her she would never go on another treasure hunt with her again. That made Gabby cry. She never thought the stained-glass piece was a murder weapon. She got caught up at the moment. But Jacqueline would have to admit something was going on. Why would someone break into their motel room?

Detective Stone brought the test results to the safehouse, and the women went over it. The police had identified the fingerprint as Anastasia's. The real puzzle was all the lead on the piece. It was in every part of the glass.

"Can we go to the house again?" asked Jacqueline.

"Why?" asked the detective.

"I think I know what killed the senator," she replied.

Gabby was intrigued but didn't say a word. She had pissed her sister off this time, and she thought she would be quiet for once.

They drove to the house in silence, parked, and went inside. Jacqueline went up to the master bedroom and started looking through the senator's closet.

"Here, this the blue-gray powder. It has no characteristic taste or smell. Too much could be deadly," said Jacqueline.

"What is it?" the detective asked.

"Lead powder. Used in making stained glass," answered Jacqueline. "It can damage the brain and nervous system, red blood cells, even the kidneys."

"What about the heart?" asked the detective.

"Maybe," replied Jacqueline.

"You know this how?" asked Stone.

Jacqueline laughed. "I'm a retired science teacher."

Detective Stone dialed her cell phone. "Pick up, Anastasia Taylor and Edith Baxter. I'll meet you back at the station." She turned to Gabby and Jacqueline. "You're free to go," she said.

"No way," Gabby said. "My sister just solved the senator's murder, and you want us to go home? Plus, you have my stained-glass piece."

Detective Stone laughed. "Ms. Bowmen, you and your sister aren't real police detectives. The stained glass is evidence. It'll be returned if, in fact, there was a murder."

"You know damn well there was a murder," Gabby said in an annoyed tone.

"You didn't seem surprised when we came to the station. I think you always questioned the senator's death. But, because his family was so powerful and wealthy, the police department did nothing."

Detective Stone was surprised at what Gabby was suggesting. But when the senator died, there was a hasty funeral and no autopsy. She had found this information out when she had gone through his case file. She knew Gabby was correct and on to something.

"Okay. You can stay and see where this new evidence points us."

Both Gabriella and Jacqueline agreed to stay.

They questioned Edith and Anastasia for several hours. Edith had broken into the women's motel room looking for the piece, but there was no conclusive evidence that either woman had a reason to harm the senator. Edith hated Anastasia but actually loved Lance Grayson. Anastasia was disturbed because Lance told her he loved someone else. The only glaring factor was the lead powder. They both had access to it.

"What about the other person he was in love with?" asked Gabby.

"No one has any idea who that is," replied Detective Stone.

"Well, let's think about this. What other job or craft would use lead powder," asked Gabby.

"How about painters and remodelers, especially of older homes?" said Jacqueline.

"I suppose you two have someone in mind," said the detective.

"We do," said the two women.

They all got back into the squad car and went off to the senator's home again. Before the detective was about to pull into the senator's long driveway, Gabby yelled, "Stop."

"What now?" said Stone.

"The next driveway," said Gabby.

They drove down a long driveway, and there it was. A Victorian house being restored, with a path to Senator Grayson's property. The front door swung open, and Garrison Taylor stepped out with his friendly rifle by his side.

"What do you want?" he yelled.

"Don't be stupid," shouted Detective Stone, as she unfastened her gun in her side holster, put her hand on the handle and raised it.

"I just want to talk," she said.

"Those two nosey women in the back seat figured it out," Garrison muttered.

He swung the rifle up, and before he could pull the trigger, he was down.

Detective Isabelle Stone was a sharpshooter, and she had only had to prove it a few times. She turned to the two women. "My question to you two is Why?"

"He was the person Senator Grayson was in love with," they replied.

CABIN 6B

Lake mist stretched over the water, resembling a smooth white blanket. The September morning sunlight reflected off the lake, producing a gradual flickering light. Isabella smiled to herself as she watched the scene unfolding in front of her. She'd never been in a cabin on a lake before. She wanted to enjoy every moment.

Sounds from the second bedroom interrupted her thoughts.

"Good morning."

Nigel and Sadie appeared in the doorway. Nigel needed to go outside to relieve himself after a night of sleep. Special Agent Nigel was a ninety-five-pound German shepherd guide dog for Special Agent Sadie Barker. Sadie's persona was that she was blind. Detective Isabella Stone was pretending to be her friend from college.

"Coffee?" Sadie said when she returned from being outside. "We need to review what we are doing today and how we will con this perp into selling us counterfeit documents."

Their person of interest was the director of the tour run by The Learn and Travel Company. The company provided tours in the United States and Europe. Isabella came across this information when a snitch made a deal for less prison time. She informed the FBI of the information, and they notified Sadie to go to work on finding who was in charge of the counterfeit ring.

Sadie had requested Isabella join her because it was in her jurisdiction. Isabella traveled to Sadie's home in Connecticut to work on the case and the snitch's information.

Isabella knew about Sadie's persona and Nigel. "What an ingenuous idea," she thought. They worked on the plan for several days and authenticated the snitch's information.

On Friday of that week, Sadie took Isabella to Harriett's tavern for margarita happy-hour to meet the Blind Justice Society women. It delighted Isabella to meet Ginny Adams and Audrey Chambers and the rest of the group of retired locals. She was astonished how they had figured out many cold cases and had accomplished outstanding detective work in their own town. They urged her to join them. She did.

Agent Baker and Detective Stone left for New Hampshire the next morning to join their tour group and apprehend the counterfeiter.

After two full cups of coffee, the women went to work. They strolled with Nigel from their cabin to the dining hall. Sadie had her dark glasses on that had a camera, a computer, and a cell phone with voice commands. Nigel wore his state-of-the-art technology service vest with a pistol in it. Isabella wore a leg holster with her service gun. Sadie's long brown hair was under a ball cap, while Isabelle's blonde hair cascaded along her shoulders. They were both dressed in jeans and hiking boots.

Seated at the back of the hall they could see everyone coming in. Sadie had arranged for her meals to be served to her by staff members. Isabella was getting her breakfast from the buffet.

Edwin Brewer, the tour coordinator, stood up and walked to the back of the hall where Sadie, Nigel and Isabella were seated. "Good morning. May I have your attention?"

Sadie recognized his slight French accent. He was a man of average height, dark hair, and olive skin. He was detailing to the group what their vacation would involve. This morning the group would stroll around the lake and look at some birds. He also introduced Sadie and Nigel, urging them not to feed or touch the dog because he was working.

Isabella took waffles and fruit and returned to the table to discover several people seated with Sadie. "I leave to get food and find a crowd has appeared, just like when we were in college," Isabella smiled.

"Everyone, Isabella my dearest friend," said Sadie.

They introduced themselves to Isabella and lingered, talking to Sadie about Nigel. Isabella squeezed between them.

When breakfast was over, the group gathered around Edwin for the two-mile hike along the lake and bird viewing. They strolled at an effortless pace, Isabella describing the scenery and birds to Sadie. Sadie's glasses were collecting pictures of the participants so she could identify them. The FBI hadn't notified the company they were investigating one of their employees because they hadn't determined how many people it involved. Sadie and Isabella had to identify all the people in the group. Sadie would send the files from today's tour to the bureau.

Edwin spoke to everyone in the group, making his way back to Sadie, Nigel, and Isabella.

"Are you enjoying the scenery?" he asked. "I wondered to myself what could a blind person see on a trip like this?" he grinned and made his way back to the head of the group.

"What was that?" Isabella asked. "Do you think he is suspicious?

"I'm not sure," replied Sadie. "Let's tell him we have a friend who requires a fraudulent passport tonight. See if he takes the bait."

As the group walked around the lake, they saw a house on a hillside through the woods. It was an elegant glass home. Everyone paused and stared. There was a well-worn path bordered by lush green grass and bushes. It continued under a canopy of trees, with light streaming through the foliage just before it curved out of sight. You could see a massive iron gate. The house had a view of the entire lake, including the cabins.

"Edwin, who owns this house?" someone asked.

He lifted his dark, thick eyebrows, frowning in obvious thought. "Mr. Elliot Ashford, the owner of the travel company. Sometimes he comes down and joins us, depending on how busy he is," explained Edwin.

"Elliott Ashford," said Isabella. "I think I read someplace that he is getting into the governor's race."

"We need to include him on our people of interest list," said Sadie.

The group made their way back to their cabins. Lunch was at one.

After lunch, everyone could do whatever they wished. Sadie, Nigel, and Isabella wondered down to the lake. Near the shore, the water was pale blue, practically translucent. The farther they peered, the darker the blue. Kayaks, canoes, and lifejackets were arranged on the waterfront.

"Let's grab a canoe and take a trip around the lake," said Sadie.

"Are you crazy?" answered Isabella.

"You'll be in the back, we'll put Nigel in the middle, and I'll be in the front. We can see what the back of the glass house looks like."

"Sounds like an insane idea, but I'm in," laughed Isabella.

They put on their lifejackets. Sadie got in, then Nigel. Isabella pushed the canoe into the water, got in, and they were off. As the breeze blew, the sun's reflections made ripples that glistened on the water. A fish broke the surface. Sadie was snapping pictures with her glasses. The canoe rounded the bend. The hilltop with the glass house came into sight. It had a large wooden boat dock with two armed guards. There was an extreme drop off from the baloney, not something you would want to fall off of. No trespassing signs were visible. Isabella kept paddling the canoe in the dock's direction.

"Slow down," said Sadie. "Nigel is going for a swim."

Before Sadie's words registered with Isabella, Nigel leaped from the canoe into the lake. He rocked the canoe, and Isabella had a challenging time controlling it. Nigel swam toward the dock. Isabella paddled fast after him and toward the not-so-friendly looking armed guards.

The guards yelled out, "Don't come any closer."

Nigel got his sleek body onto the wooden dock. He shook his thick fury ninety-five-pound wet body over the men. Isabella gradually brought the canoe to a stop at the dock.

"This is private property," said one guard. "Can't you two read the signs?"

"My dog loves to swim. I'm sorry," said Sadie. All the time she was collecting pictures of them and their holstered pistols.

Knowing it would be impossible to get the dog back into the canoe, Sadie yelled. "Swim."

Nigel jumped back into the water. The men pushed the canoe out into the lake.

"Don't come this way again," the heavier one said. "Next time I'll have you arrested."

When they were a fair distance away. Isabella said, "Sadie, please tell me when you plan to do something like that. I nearly had a heart attack."

As they paddled back to the shore, Nigel swam alongside the canoe. They spotted one of the women from the tour group coming from the vicinity of the glass house with Edwin. She was a slim, middle-aged, silver-haired woman who was yelling at him. They couldn't hear what she was saying, but it was obvious by the way she was waving her hands in the air that she was upset.

"We need to find out about that. Maybe she requested phony documents," laughed Sadie.

"She could have tried to meet Elliot Ashford," replied Isabella.

"Why?" replied Sadie.

"He is single, rich, and lives in a glass house!" laughed Isabella. "What more could you want?"

They got the canoe to shore and returned the lifejackets. Edwin came hustling down the waterfront to meet them. He had somehow gotten away from the woman.

"You two need to stay away from Mr. Ashford's home. I received a call from him. Makes me wonder if you aren't paparazzi or something," he said in a heightened tone. He swiveled around and marched away, kicking up sand.

"We got on someone's nerve," said Sadie.

They strolled back to their cabin to shower and get ready for dinner. Sadie sent the files to the bureau of the glass house and guards.

"We can go over the information I sent when we return from dinner," said Sadie. Wandering to the dining hall, the silvery-haired woman that was perturbed earlier was walking in the glass house's direction.

"She doesn't give up. Or maybe she has a date with Ashford," chuckled Isabella.

During dinner, two women from the tour group came to their table to talk about their friend Amelia. She had been invited to Ashford's for cocktails. Amelia was positive she recognized him from a business deal gone bad.

Sadie and Isabella were struggling not to show too much interest. Both were curious, but they needed to get on with the case they were working. They made mental notes of the women's nametags. Betty and Linda were their names. But tonight, the plan was to speak with Edwin about a family member who needed papers to get into the United States. After dinner, Isabella would approach him.

"Edwin, can I speak to you alone?" Isabella asked.

"Yes," my dear.

"Angel Castro is my relative," she said. He was really the informer.

"I don't think I recall hearing that name," Edwin replied.

"Sure, you do," replied Isabella. "You made papers for him a few months ago. You remember? I need another set for a different family member, or Angel might turn you into the police. Speak to him if you don't trust me." She dialed her phone and passed it to him.

Edwin listened, his eyes widening as Angel talked to him. When the conversation was done, he handed Isabella the phone. "I have to check with my boss about this. Have the information ready in the morning. Does your friend understand that she is traveling with a criminal?"

"I'm here to help Sadie. She isn't involved in my business. Her being blind with a guide dog allows me to do many things," Isabella answered.

Sadie and Nigel strolled along the lake, making their way to the cabin to wait for Isabella. She returned a few minutes after they arrived.

"Well, he is working on my papers. He had to ask his boss," said Isabella.

"I wonder who the boss is?" said Sadie.

"We have his phone tapped, and an officer is keeping him under surveillance," replied Isabella.

"Great job. I understood your locals weren't as good as the FBI," laughed Sadie.

There was a knock on the cabin door.

"Who is it?" Sadie asked.

"Amelia's friends from dinner tonight," Betty and Linda.

Sadie opened the door, and the two women rushed inside.

"Amelia hasn't returned, and she hasn't answered her phone. It keeps going to voicemail. We're worried. Amelia told us that Elliot had cheated her out of money."

"Why are you coming to us with this?" asked Isabella.

"You have been so nice to us. We just didn't know who to go to," said Betty.

"I think you should find Edwin and tell him," said Sadie.

"We looked for him. He has just disappeared!"

Just then a long, wailing sound pierced the stillness of the night. They could hear sirens in the distance.

Betty and Linda stood up and rushed for the door.

Isabella's phone buzzed. It was the officer that had been following Edwin. There had been an accident at the glass house. Someone had fallen off the baloney into the rugged ravine below. He didn't know who the victim was yet.

Isabella sighed. "There has been an accident at the glass house. They need everyone to return to your cabins so they can take a head count."

Betty and Linda didn't question who had given Isabella this information. They excused themselves and left.

Sadie asked, "Who was on the phone?"

"The officer following Edwin," Isabella said. "Edwin received a phone call that was being traced, but it was a prepaid phone. They have a general location. It's the cabin area."

"We need to deal with this carefully," said Sadie.

They glanced outside, and everyone was being asked to go back to their cabin. The whole area was a crime scene now. Edwin had vanished.

Sadie sat down next to Nigel and petted his soft, thick fur. Something was out-of-the-ordinary.

"What are you thinking?" asked Isabella

"The prepaid phone. Ashford wouldn't have one. Why would Amelia?" Sadie replied.

"So, who did Edwin talk to," asked Isabella.

"That's what we need to find out," said Sadie. Her phone rang. It was her boss, Special Agent White.

"Stand down," he said. "I don't want Isabella or your cover blown. The locals will handle this case."

"I have one question," said Sadie. "Who is in the ravine?"

"Don't know yet. They haven't gotten to them," he replied.

"Isabella, we are to stand down," Sadie said.

"No way," said Isabella. "We've come too far to let an accident get in our way."

"Orders," replied Sadie.

"I don't take orders from the FBI."

"Good," said Sadie. "Now let's solve this case."

Sadie went on her computer and looked up Amelia's profile. Then Betty and Linda's. The three silver foxes had a collection of charges against them. Somehow, they always seemed to get out of them. But now the feds were looking at them for computer fraud.

One of their marks was a business partner of Elliott Ashford. The partner was into them for a hefty sum of money and Ashford got him out of it.

"But how does Edwin fit into all of this?" asked Isabella.

"Maybe the ladies are into counterfeiting too, "said Sadie.

"Let me call my snitch and see if he can shed some light on this," replied Isabella.

"Angel, it's your favorite friend, Detective Stone," said Isabella. "Do you know anything about three women and Edwin? I'll take care of you, just tell me."

Isabella smiled as she listened to Angel tell her about the women. She hung up and turned to Sadie.

"Betty was the one involved with Ashford's friend. The three women hacked his computer and got into his bank accounts. When Ashford found out about the hacking, he had gangster type men pay them a visit. They were out a huge sum of money," said Isabella. "Edwin is a two-bit criminal, and they hooked up with him to get Ashford. They think he is the leader of the counterfeit ring."

"My head is whirling," said Sadie. "Too many criminals in one place."

Suddenly there was a hollow echo of knuckles rapping at the cabin door. Isabella answered the door with her gun in her hand in her pocket.

It was one of local officers from the station, "Just checking to see that you two are okay. Can I come in?" he asked.

"Who's in the ravine?" asked Isabella.

"Not who, but how many," he replied.

Sadie stared at Isabella in disbelief.

THE COVE

Claudia Carson gazed out over the calmly moving water. The surrounding trees swayed in the wind as if moving to a melody. Life was simple this day — four tanned young women in the water, two in kayaks, two on paddleboards. She heard laughter skipping across the water like a thrown pebble. An older gray-haired woman sat with her dog on the deck, soaking her feet. Birds passing overhead. This scene wasn't always the case on the cove.

Claudia's dark, almost black eyes filled with tears. They flowed down the cheeks of her olive skin. An accident? Or murder. She never accepted that Logan, her husband, drowned. The water in this cove always calm, never over your head anywhere. It made little sense.

Logan, a retired Navy SEAL: How could *he* have drowned?

Claudia returned this summer to ease her mind, one-way or the other. She rented the same cabin, the same boats, and all the other equipment for the same time. Claudia planned ongoing through different scenarios until something made sense out of what had happened on the cove last July. She hoped to do all of this with no one noticing. As she stood there, she could see a woman in her mid-forties, with chestnut hair approaching her. It was Ginger Hollister, the owner of the cabins.

"How are you?" asked Ginger.

"Taking it one day at a time. You know."

Claudia had never cared for Ginger. The woman would always flirt with Logan, annoying her. It had always caused her to wonder if Logan had known Ginger before. There was something about their body language together. It was as if they had their own little secret code. When she'd asked Logan that question, he laughed.

"To be honest, I had a tough year," said Claudia. "I kept pushing myself forward to get things done. The estate work took most of my time, and now I'm figuring out what to do on my next journey in life. Logan and I worked as detectives for so long. I never thought about what would happen if one of us died before the other."

"Life's funny, like that," said Ginger.

"How so?" asked Claudia irritated.

"Not planning."

"I still can't accept Logan drowned."

"Why?". "Even the best swimmers have accidents."

"Not Logan," Claudia said as she turned and walked back toward her cabin. Sitting down on the couch, she sobbed, it grew louder and more violent, shaking her whole body. Claudia laid down and tried to get herself under control. Gradually calming her breathing down and drifting off to sleep.

Logan appeared calling her name. She was on the deck, and he was in the water. Tempting her to come in.

"Come on in its beautiful," he yelled.

She could hear herself saying. "I have to finish what I'm work-ing on." Claudia gazed at the people on the cove. Two blonde young boys in red kayaks with their parents, two men waiting to go into the water, one man having a problem getting into the kayak with his prosthetic leg, the other one helping him.

The men turned their attention to Logan in the water and yelled something to him. Logan moved toward them. He appeared to be arguing with them. "Logan," she cried out, and suddenly came this sweet-smelling odor and darkness.

Claudia woke with a jolt of air, inflating her lungs. It took a few minutes for her to get her bearings. She realized she had fallen asleep and drifted back to that day in July.

Was Logan trying to tell her something? Had she seen the crime and not remembered? Did she see the killers?

"Logan," she yelled out. "Say something to me," Silence in the room. It was such a vivid dream, details she had not remembered before from that day. But why? Time to be a detective.

Claudia rose and walked to the kitchen where she made herself a stiff gin and tonic. Her eyes scanned the room, and there in the corner was Logan's briefcase. She hadn't wanted to look at it before, but she brought it because Logan always had it with him. Now she sensed that it was time for her to go through it. Slowly, she put the combination into the keypad. It didn't work. Claudia was sure of the numbers, he always used her birthday. Once again, she tapped the numbers in. It popped opened. Peering inside, there were file folders and notes from Logan's cases. Claudia put the folders on the kitchen table. She continued searching the briefcase, looking in each compartment, then feeling something in the lining. Gripping a knife, she cut it out. To her surprise, a flash drive. Claudia walked over to the laptop and turned it on, inserted it, and tried to open it. Password-protected. She attempted many combinations of letters and numbers. The files wouldn't open. Frustrated, she walked over to the front door to get some fresh summer air and pull herself together. Sauntering toward the cabin was Ginger.

"Hi, she said. "Are you okay?"

"Yes, why would you ask that?"

"Your red eyes give you away. Let this go. Logan died, and you have to move on. If you don't, it will eat you up. Let's get out of here and have something to eat," suggested Ginger.

"Good idea," said Claudie.

Harriet's tavern was loud, noisy, crowded, and filled with a rich aroma of the different varieties of seafood, fries, and burgers. They sat at the bar, getting drinks and something to eat. They talked while they eat and ordered several rounds of drinks. When they got up to leave, Claudia felt lightheaded when she stood up. Balancing herself on the barstool.

"Lightweight," Ginger laughed.

As they made their way to the door, two men came in one with an outstanding jerky gait. The other was bearded with a thick mop of grey hair. They sat at the bar. Claudia recognized them from her dream. They had been the ones arguing with Logan.

"Do you know who those guys are?" she asked Ginger.

"Why, you interested?" Ginger said with a smile on her face.

"No, I've seen them hanging around," Claudia lied.

"They're locals; they work on the dock. I know they had been arrested a few times."

"For what?" asked Claudia.

"Marijuana, pills. You know, stupid stuff. Logan monitored them. You must have known that," said Ginger as if she was asking a question.

"Was that a question?" asked Claudia. "We didn't always talk about our cases."

"Hard to believe," Ginger said.

"It's true," shot back Claudia.

They walked back to the cabin in silence.

"Thanks, Ginger, I needed that."

Ginger waved her hand and continued to her cabin. Claudia went right to Logan's files on the table where she had left them. She realized she had never talked to him about that case. Why? Ginger was right. They had talked about almost everything? Maybe Logan feared for her safety, or was it something he didn't want her to know about?

Claudia brought the files to bed. She looked at them for a short time, and her eyelids got heavy; she fell asleep. Her breathing became shallow, then darkness.

Claudia sensed a presence in her deep sleep, then a sweet-smelling odor; a struggle, then her body letting go and darkness without thought, as if the world no longer existed.

The sound of a motorboat in the distance brought her back to the light. She sat up in bed, causing the folders to scatter over the floor. Her thoughts were scrambled. Was it a dream or something buried deep in her memory?

Coffee, that's what she needed. Claudia climbed out of bed and staggered to the kitchen to make some. Her head was throbbing, and she felt nauseous. Had she drank too much last night? Gripping a bottle of aspirin, she poured coffee into a cup and slipped out onto the deck to glance over the cove. What had happened during the night? Claudia could remember being sleepy, but her body seemed to struggle with a presence and that sweet-smelling odor. What did all this mean? Was there a memory in her head that needed to get out? She was puzzled and realized she needed to figure out the answers.

Moving back into the bedroom, she gathered up the folders from the floor and then retrieved the flash drive. Logan was so organized he would surely have the information … unless someone had stolen it. She labored through the folders, only taking the time to make more coffee and have cheese and crackers. The last folder was out of order, not like the other ones. Claudia put the papers together by dates and started piecing the case together. Things were missing, like pictures and surveillance notes. Logan would have never put a file together in this order. Someone must have gone through them. But who?

Claudia had taken the files home with her last year and never looked at them until now. Who would have known or even cared about them? Ginger came to her mind right away. That's why she had been coming around and dinner last night at Harriett's tavern. Then Claudia thought about the two guys from the bar last night. It had to be them.

Claudia dressed quickly. She wanted to take a walk on the beach and clear her foggy liquor-soaked brain. As she walked on the beach the grainy, sand shaped her feet. The comfort of the gentle sound of the water and the rhythmic movement helped free her mind. As she walked back to her cabin, she noticed something sticking out from the surrounding latticework of a cabin. Curious, she scrolled over the cabin. A rag was hanging out of the opening. She tugged at it pulling it out of latticework. It had a familiar sweet-smell like her dream. Chloroform!

Someone had drugged her last night and perhaps even the day Logan had died. But why? The flash drive must hold the answer; she had to get it open. Rushing back to the cabin, exhausted and still fighting the throbbing headache she determined to figure this out. She was a police detective she had cases like this. Think, she said out loud, what are you missing. Just then a knock on the screen door; Claudia could see the chestnut hair of Ginger. Damn, she thought.

"Can I come in?"

"Sure," Claudia said rolling her eyes.

"I wanted to see how you were doing after last night. You had a lot to drink. I know this is hard for you. But you need to move on, Claudia. You need to accept Logan's death."

Claudia looked right at Ginger with her dark eyes and the pain in her chest from her broken heart. "I don't have to do anything!" Claudia said, almost yelling. "I think someone in this cove murdered Logan." She couldn't believe she had let her feelings, out to Ginger.

"You're crazy, said Ginger. "Your snooping around is bad for business. I want you out of here by Friday!"

"No," said Claudia. "I paid for two weeks, and that's how long I'm staying."

"I'll return all your money," shouted Ginger.

"Get out. I'm not leaving!"

Ginger stood up. "By Friday," she said as she stormed out of the cabin.

Claudia gathered her thoughts, made a drink, and continued out onto the deck. The velvety darkness seemed terrifying, yet inviting simultaneously. One - by-one, small points of light started popping up in the sky. If only she could figure out the password to the flash-drive, she thought. Claudia thought about the cases Logan and her had worked on. Then it came to her, she remembered a case Logan had a long time ago. He left out page numbers in his file to make a code. Lifting her drink and going into the cabin, she looked over the last case. Noticing the missing page numbers, she put them into the computer. The file opened.

There were pictures of a woman and a young boy who looked familiar. Why did she recognize them? Claudia kept going through the files. A news article about a young man that lost his leg after a car chase. The detective on the case, Logan. The young boy was the man in the bar. But why did he hide all this and not tell her? What if the young man in the photo was the small boy in the picture with the women? Claudia enlarged the photograph; Ginger and the man in the bar. Could he be Ginger's and Logan's son? Is this the secret? She made another drink and continued to go through the file. It took late into the night for Claudia to map out all the evidence she needed to make a case. Exhaustion was ebbing in, her thoughts were inconsistence, Claudia needed to get some rest. Making another drink before she stumbled into bed intoxicated.

Waking early and struggling to get out of bed to continue her daunting task of proving the murderer of her beloved husband Logan. She had to make a discussion whether to call her detective society or Logan's teammates. Claudia made a call to one member of Logan's Seal team to discuss the evidence. It would take a day for them to get what they needed and make their way to the cove. They scheduled their arrival for the next evening at nine o'clock that would give Claudia time to gather more evidence. She went back to the files and computer and worked slowly gathering more proof than she had done the night before. This time she did it sober.

Avoiding Ginger, the next day until her guest would arrive after dark, Claudia didn't want questions. Nine o'clock that evening, four men knocked on the door of Claudia's cabin. They realized that criminal deception and drug dealing had been the reason that they had killed Logan. The team was also there because of the attacks on Claudia. Logan's Seal brothers were ready to uphold the legacy of their teammate.

Claudia and the team made their way down to Ginger's cabin. The group stayed in the shadows while she crept onto the porch. She heard raised voices coming from the cabin. Peeking into the window, Claudia spied Ginger and the two men from the bar inside.

"I tell you she knows. We have to stop her," said the man with the prosthetic leg.

"I told her to leave by Friday," said Ginger. "We don't want another accident on this cove."

"She won't leave unless it's in a pine box," said the man. "You should have taken care of her when you had the chance in her cabin last summer, or the other night; when you chloroformed her.

"He laughed."

Ginger glared at him. "You may be my son, but I can take care of you too," she said with an icy stare. "You're the one who drugged Logan and drowned him. I didn't have any part of that. I'll tell the police that too," said Ginger.

"Logan was a smart guy. He figured out how I use my leg to carry drugs. Then figuring out you were the head of this drug business on the cove. He was getting ready to arrest all of us. And you're the one who lied to him for twenty years that he's my father. He only found out when I lost my leg ... by my blood type. You gave me the stuff to put in his drink to knock him out so we could drown him," he laughed. "That's what I'll tell the police."

Claudia leaned against the wooden shingles, struggling to hold back her tears. She wanted to scream out, her heart filled with pain. For that single moment she thought what she had planned was wrong. Then that thought was gone. Gun in hand, she stood there for a moment then signaled the team. She wanted revenge for Logan's death.

The armed men came out of hiding and surrounded Claudia. Eight eyes in the darkness looking into her soul. She nodded they kicked in the door, surprising the three inside. Claudia stepped inside the cabin. She pointed her weapon at them.

You're under arrest for the murderer of Logan Carson.

"Who the hell are these guys," asked Ginger

"Logan's Seal team," Claudia answered.

The grey hair guy said. "They didn't come here to arrest us.

Claudia laughed the man straight faced and weapons pointed.

"You won't kill us," said Ginger. "You're a cop."

Claudia replied. "You're right, I would never kill you. But my friends want to give you swimming lessons."

THE FACE IN THE WINDOW

"Mirror, mirror on the wall who's the happiest woman of them all?" Wavy brown-haired, blue-eyed Tina Ryan stared at herself, tears running down her face. "What's wrong with me?" she thought. "They have offered me the job of a lifetime."

Tina would be the new financial director of the Homewood Retirement Community, the largest retirement center in the state of Connecticut. All that was left was telling Winston, her boss, that she would leave in a month.

Winston was a middle-aged man with crow's feet around his green eyes. His face was time-worn and wrinkled. He devoted himself to teaching her how to be a top seller in real estate. But life goes on, and Tina needed this change. She had a few house transactions to close, then she would leave. Winston took everything personally. Tina was positive he would feel she was disloyal.

The drive to the office this morning seemed more tedious than usual. Tina went straight to her desk when she got to work. Winston called her into his office. Could he have found out about the new job? She knew what she would say. Tina had rehearsed it many times since she took the new position. "Don't be nervous," she told herself.

Winton's office had piles of real estate listings everywhere, on the floor, his table, his desk, any place he could put them. He had a computer, but he always preferred having a hard copy of everything.

"We have a new listing at 99 Lincoln Drive," said Winston.

"The Gibson house?" asked Tina.

"Yes," he responded.

"I loved that house when I was a child. It looked so beautiful," she said.

"'Was' is the keyword," he said, raising his winter-white eyebrows.

"What does that mean?" Tina asked.

"It's been ignored for years. There was also a suicide in that house," replied Winston.

"Who?" questioned Tina.

"The young Gibson boy, Matthew. He jumped from the fourth-floor landing."

"I don't recall ever learning about that," replied Tina.

"You know, money can influence anyone's actions. Maybe they paid to keep it hushed. Money talks," he sneered.

Tina rolled her blue eyes.

"The press said he jumped. But everybody knew he had issues. Even his sister hated him. Claire, the owner, thinks her brother's ghost – correction – 'adopted' brother's ghost haunts the place. She made sure she told me that. He was a disturbed little boy who the family shouldn't have adopted," Winston said. I think she was 16 when he died. In fact, there was gossip that she might have pushed him to his death."

Tina couldn't believe what Winston was telling her. She was tongue-tied.

"So, you want me to look at the listing?" she asked in an irritated tone.

"It will take creative work since the house is being sold as-is. You have a small budget, not enough to do much," said Winston.

"I'll go there this morning," said Tina. "What price range do they want?"

"She'll leave that up to us."

Tina grabbed the folder for the listing and left the office. She drove to 99 Lincoln Drive, steering up the unkempt driveway. It wasn't like the formerly glamorous home it had been. The dead grass littered the lawn. Overgrown trees with dried brown leaves hung in irregular shapes. The house and the garage both needed a good painting, the paint weathered and peeling off at a rapid pace. Second-floor windows were broken, and the dirty ones seemed to stare at her. It was as if they dared her to step inside.

A flock of blackbirds landed on the wires above the house, gathering together and eyeing her. The birds just stared down at her. She could feel her pulse beating in her ears, blocking out all other sounds except the ragged breath moving in and out of her mouth at regular, gasping intervals. Tina wondered if she should go into the house. If the outside looked like this, what horrors awaited her inside?

She stepped onto the broken stairs and opened the door. It made a disturbing, creaking noise. Cobwebs and spider webs dangled here and there. She saw a mouse dart across the floor. Not at all the way she had imagined it looked when she was younger.

Tina remembered how grand the house had looked in those days. The phone rang, startling her. She went into the living room and glanced around for it. There was an old rotary phone on the sill of the front window. She made her way over and picked it up.

"Hello," she said. No answer, just a hellish sounding noise on the other end. A static mix with faint screaming cries. It was unnerving. It happened several more times. Tina thought maybe it was Winston playing a joke. She would make sure to get it disconnected when she returned to the office.

A deep and menacing noise from upstairs caught her attention. "Should I go up the wooden staircase?" she thought. This listing was getting hair-raising. In fact, the hair on her neck had risen several times. Climbing the large wooden staircase, she stopped and looked up at the magnificent Tiffany glass cupola. A beacon of light pierced through the panes of the dirty glass. The sunlight bathed the dust-covered black and white tiles on the floor in the foyer. It was hypnotic. Tina had the feeling of spinning. She squeezed her eyes shut to stop the feeling, then opened them back up.

She started once more up the wooden staircase, pausing on the first floor. There were three bedrooms and two full bathrooms. Dust lay over every surface, resembling dirty snow. The air was thick. Dried mold and filthy dust collected on the mirrors, and the smell of musty mildew hung in the air. As she entered one bedroom, Tina noticed how everything looked as if someone still lived there. Pictures, bedding, and clothing lay everywhere. It all needed a good cleaning.

The phone rang downstairs again and continued ringing.

"I should check out the rest of the floors," Tina thought. She found the same bedding and clothing, dust, and stale air. Everything would need to be removed. She climbed to the fourth floor. The glass cupola loomed above her head. Light streamed down at her. She leaned over and looked at the foyer below. It was a long way down. Matthew Gibson had jumped to his death from here... or maybe not. Tina wanted to know the answer to that question.

Icy air whirled around her head. Tina heard a child's voice pleading ever so quietly in the cold air. Perhaps the wind? No, that wasn't correct. Another chilly breeze whipped around her.

A soft child's voice whispered, "Help me!" She felt a gentle tap on her shoulder and jumped. Tina, terrified, sprung to her feet and darted down the staircase. Her foot slipped and turned outward, and before she knew it, she was on her back. As she slid down the hardwood stairs, pain flashed across her lower back. Tina grasped the railing and stopped herself on the last staircase. She struggled to her feet. She straightened her clothes, smoothed her brown wavy hair and took a deep breath. Shaken, she fled the house. "What lost soul dwelled in that place?" Tina thought, horrified.

Tina got into her car and drove down the driveway. Looking back at the house, she spotted a young boy's face in the window, staring out at her from the second story. It was as real as if he were sitting next to her in the car. She slammed on the brakes and blinked. She gazed back at the window. The image had disappeared.

She drove straight to the office, parked, and went in. When Winston saw her, he asked what she thought about the listing. Tina didn't want to tell him. He would think she was crazy. Tina's entire body ached from the fall, and she knew it would be bruised. Before she said anything, she needed to calm down the anxiety that curled in her stomach, choking her throat and not letting any words out.

"That house requires an abundance of work," said Tina. "When was the last time someone lived there?"

"Years ago. The daughter inherited it. That's all I know," said Winston.

"The house will need work and cleaning," said Tina.

"I'll call the client and set up a meeting," said Winston.

"The first thing we have to do is to get that damn phone shut off," said Tina.

"Okay," he answered.

It relieved Winston that Tina was taking the listing. He had gone to the house, and it had given him the creeps. "A grown man afraid," Winston thought. He didn't want Tina to know he had been there. Winston had dashed out of the house and driven down the driveway like someone had been chasing him. But he needed that listing and the commission it would bring. He was just trying to keep his business together, and the money this sale would bring would help. Winston knew Tina could put the contract together.

The next day, Tina's amateur sleuth went to work. Her first stop was the town hall to look at the files about Matthew's death. She explained to the clerk sitting at her desk that she had the listing on the house and needed background information. She spent the morning reading what seemed to be, as she would say, a cover-up.

Matthew was Mr. Gibson's son by another woman. Beatrice Gibson had been given a generous sum of money to accept Matthew as her son. In most people's eyes, she treated him like a son. Claire was told he was adopted, not that Matthew was her half-brother. She despised him. He had been injured several times and always when she was watching him. The excuse was an accident, something he did. There was a note in the files about the children's blood types. That got Tina's attention. The children had unique kinds. She thought that was odd.

Matthew's blood didn't match anyone else's in the Gibson family. All the blood types were in the police files, even the other woman's. She made a note of it. It seemed impossible to Tina that Matthew was Mr. Gibson's son.

The third floor of the town hall housed the property records.

The house had been in the Gibson family for over two hundred years, and it seemed odd to Tina that Claire would want to sell it. Unless she was trying to cover something up. Tina hoped Winston had the meeting with Claire set up so she could ask her key questions.

The next day Tina went to the historical society office to look into their archives. The frumpily dressed woman at the front desk happily helped. She told Tina that another adolescent man named Jacob Gibson had committed suicide in that house. A rumor circulated that a spirit had possessed him, that he had run up the stairs and flew off the railing to his death. Matthew's death was in the same month and the same day. Supposedly, a spirit had told him to jump too.

Tina didn't know what to make of all this information. She wondered if the voice she was hearing might be the spirit itself.

She remembered reading in the police files that Claire had told the same story. "Had Claire read it in some place?" Tina wondered. Perhaps someone told her to say that? Had she plotted to take Matthew's life on the same day, so it looked like a spirit had possessed him? Or was that house haunted? Tina knew she heard the voice of a child whispering for help up on the fourth floor.

Just then, her cell phone rang. It was Winston. "Hello," said Tina.

"We have a meeting at four o'clock this afternoon with Claire. Where are you?"

"Getting background information for the listing," she replied. "I'll be there soon."

Tina drove up the unkempt driveway with overgrown weeds and unwanted plants. She found a spot to park. She walked up the stairs onto the rickety porch. Opening the creaking door, she stepped into the grand hallway. Tina gazed up at the dome on the top of the fourth floor. She drew a deep breath and shouted, "What secrets do you hold? Show me a sign!"

The door slammed behind her, and the phone started ringing. Tina wondered if she had made the right decision to come alone. She started up the stairs, then stopped. A child singing a song was coming from the basement. Tina went downstairs. They had built an amphitheater of sorts. Dusty velvet drapes hung down, framing the door. She tugged them apart. A flow of icy air embraced her, sending a chill up her spine. Tina searched and found family items: old magazines, knitting, and a family album covered with thick dust. The album contained many Gibson family members. Someone had taken the time to write names on several of them.

She found a picture of Matthew as a small child. He was the face in the window. There was one of Jacob. The two looked nothing alike. Matthew didn't resemble any of the Gibson family.

Suddenly, the pages of the album started flipping of its own volition, moving faster and faster until it stopped at a picture of a young woman. Her long, wavy hair fell to her shoulders. An angelic smile lit up her face. The woman stood at the top of the stairs next to a man. She was holding Matthew in her arms. A cold breeze whirled around Tina, causing her to jump back. "This is all so weird," she thought. She yanked the picture of the woman out from the album and stuffed it into her purse. She wondered if it might be Claire.

Something upstairs scurried across the floor. Tina crept over to the stairs, feeling trapped. There was only one way out of the basement – up the stairs where the sounds were coming from. She made her way up to the main floor. A squirrel was running around in the living room. "It must have come in through the attic," she thought. This house needed a new roof. Tina would have to capture the varmint at some point. She had other concerns now. Tina had to get back to the office for her meeting with Claire. Rushing out of the house, Tina got into her car and down the driveway. She glanced back at the second floor. Matthew was in the window. She stopped and stared up.

"I'll find out what happened to you," Tina promised.

She drove over the speed limit to get to the office. Tina went right to Winston's office.

"Hi," he said.

"What does Claire look like?" she asked. "Or better yet," she reached into her purse, "Is this Claire?"

"No, that isn't Claire," answered Winston.

"The family album flipped to this picture," she said with a frightened tone.

He stared at her like she was crazy, but then he remembered how frightened he, too, had been at the house. "Maybe taking this listing wasn't such a brilliant idea," he thought. But it was too late. Claire would soon be at the office.

Tina's eyes widened, and she took a step backward when Claire arrived at the office. She was a stunning blonde woman dressed impeccably with kindness in her smile. Claire explained that after her parent's death, she had traveled. Claire didn't want the house and should have sold it a long time ago. Now she just wanted to get rid of it.

"Claire, the house needs cleaning and cosmetic work," said Tina. "You will have to invest some money to get a good return."

"I am not interested in doing that," said Claire. "I'll have the house cleaned out, but that will be it. I want that house gone."

Tina said she understood and would get her a price for having the cleaning done. "I would like to ask you a few questions about this house."

"Like what?" said Claire in a soft voice.

"Why hasn't the phone been disconnected?" said Tina. She drew a long breath, "Is this house... haunted?"

Claire laughed. "I disconnect the phone. There have been rumors for years that my adopted brother haunts the house. Even strange noises and faces in the window. I'm not sure I believe any of that."

Tina took the picture she had stuffed in her purse out. "Do you know who this woman is?"

"Yes, it's my Aunt Margaret. My mother's younger sister. Why?" questioned Claire.

Tina made up a story of finding it next to a picture of Matthew.

"Give me a few days, and I'll get back to you with all the information about the house," said Tina.

Tina went on her computer as soon as Claire left. She needed to search for Claire's mother's obituary to find out Margaret's last name. Margaret lived in the retirement home that Tina's new job was at. Time for a visit to Homewood Retirement Estates.

The nurse at the front desk said nothing at first when Tina asked to see Margaret. She then told her Margaret had dementia and a hard time recognizing people.

"May I please see her," asked Tina.

Margaret's private room was a pale blue with wood-finished floors. She smiled and greeted Tina.

"Do I know you, dear?" she asked.

"No," replied Tina. "I'm working here soon, and I thought I would meet some patients."

"That's nice," Margaret said.

She was a tiny, frail, grey-haired woman. She had pictures of two children and a man on her dresser. The photos of Claire and Matthew hung on the wall. Tina knew the man wasn't Mr. Gibson, but she thought she recognized him. Not one picture of her sister. That seemed odd. Tina picked up the set of photos and asked Margaret who they were.

"My son, niece, and the love of my life," she said. "My son died a horrible death," she blurted out and then cried.

"I'm sorry if I upset you," Tina said.

Tina glanced at the pictures again and recognized the man. She was replacing him at the retirement home. Mr. Alexander. He was a handsome man, slender, with piercing eyes. Even though this was an older picture, she was sure it was him. Something about the eyes. Just then, Mr. Alexander came into the room.

"May I ask why you are here?" He sounded irritated as he paced back and forth in the room. "Please step out into the hallway."

She did as he asked.

"This patient is not to have any visitors. She's dangerous."

"Margaret doesn't appear dangerous to me," replied Tina. "In fact, I feel she is just lonely."

"I thought we agreed on no patient contact," he scolded. "Why were you visiting, anyway?"

Tina turned around and walked back into the room, grabbed her coat, and walked out without answering his questions. "Do I want to work here?" she thought. Tina drove out of the facility

and decided to take one more look at the pictures in the album
and the house.

Tina parked on a side street and walked over to the house.
She entered the house. It was icy cold, and there was an eeriness
in the air. She hustled downstairs to look through the album.
There was a picture of Margaret, Matthew, and Mr. Alexander.
He was Matthew's father. Matthew had those same piercing eyes.
That's the discrepancy in the blood type. Matthew wasn't Mr.
Gibson's son. "Why pretend? Why adopt him?" she wondered.
Margaret was the other woman, but Mr. Gibson was not the
father. Did he not know that in the beginning? Did he not know
about Mr. Alexander?

An icy breeze embraced her as if somebody was pulling her
up the stairs to the dome. She heard it. The soft, childlike whisper, "Help me."

Tina started up the stairs to the dome. As she stared at it, she
heard the creaking door downstairs open. She rushed into the
room beside the dome and hid in the closet, leaving the door
ajar so she could watch anyone who entered the hallway through
the mirror.

Footsteps were climbing the stairs. Mr. Alexander appeared
in the mirror. He entered the room and sat in an old rocking chair.
He cradled his arms as though holding a baby. Mr. Alexander
started singing softly and crying. "I will always be here for you,
my sweet son, Matthew. Don't cry." The house moaned and
made sharp, loud, cracking sounds like thunder. Tina's heart-
beat rapidly. She was sweating. Just then, her cell phone rang. Mr.
Alexander jumped up and whipped the door open.

"What are you doing here?" he screamed at her.

Tina didn't answer. She tried getting around him. He took a
step forward, crowding her. They struggled like wrestlers, moving

back and forth, going through the doorway, landing up under the dome. The icy air spun around them, making whistling noises. They continued wrestling, and pushing and pulling each other. They landed at the fourth-floor railing. Tina pushed with force and got away from him.

"You killed your son, Matthew!" she shouted at him.

"No, the Gibson family killed him. They would never let me have him," he said, breathless from grappling with Tina. He grabbed for her but lost his balance. She again pushed him as hard as she could. Mr. Alexander tumbled over the railing, landing on the black and white tile floor below. Tina ran down the stairs. The police busted through the door as she reached the first floor.

"How did you know?" Tina asked.

"A 911 dispatcher said a child kept repeating, 'a woman needs help,'" one officer replied.

The phone rang one more time.

THE JUDGEMENT

The hinges of the heavy wooden door of the courthouse were silent. No more groaning. Dull white walls that required paint and a proper cleaning surrounded the Hall of Justice, except for one sizeable brown water spot that the accused, Tinker Wiley, had been peering at for the last four weeks. They charged her with killing her colleague, Dr. Daniel Bradford, the lover of her childhood friend Billy Franklin. Tinker had threatened him in public. Now the whole courtroom waited for her peers to deliver their verdict. Eight middle-aged men, seven white and one black, and four gray-haired women with skin as white as snowflakes. Tinker thought, "How can these people be my peers?" A prominent black civil rights lawyer for a father and a white socialite mother. The honey-wheat-skinned Tinker had been battling her entire life to fit in. Could she get justice in a southern court? She could hope.

Everyone stood up as the jury entered. Not one juror established eye contact with the defense table. The black-robed judge cleared his throat.

"Mr. Foreman, have you arrived at a verdict?" he asked.

"Your Honor, we have," the stout white foreman responded.

The bailiff walked over to get the folded verdict paper from the foreman and handed it to the judge. He read it, expressionless, then handed it back to the bailiff. He gave it to the court clerk.

"How say you?" she asked.

"We, the jury, find Doctor Tinker Wiley guilty of voluntary manslaughter with mitigating circumstances," the foreman replied.

"Members of the jury, listen to your verdict as it stands recorded. You say you find the defendant, Doctor Tinker Wiley, guilty. And so, say you all?" the court clerk asked.

"Yes," acknowledged the jurors.

The judge called her name. "Tinker Wiley, please stand."

Her lawyer slipped her arm under Tinker's and supported her as she rose. She stood with her feet glued to the floor, burning tears rolling down her face. How could these jurors fail to determine that she hadn't killed Dr. Bradford? She had wanted to, maybe. She had gone to his office and threatened him. In the end, she couldn't do it. Her inner voice called for her to yell at everyone in the courtroom, "I'm innocent! Why don't you understand that?"

The judge addressed Tinker. "Miss Wiley, you'll return in two weeks for your sentencing. You may remain on bail under house arrest."

Tinker's father called in some favors from people he had helped in the past. They reciprocated because they owed him. They convinced the judge to allow her to be on house arrest and bail. There were mitigating factors surrounding the case concerning Tinker's mental state at the time of the crime. These factors could allow the court to reduce the charges and lessen the jail time.

Tinker sat in the chair. Tears rolled down her cheeks, one after another, until there was a steady stream of salty tears flowing down her face. Her lawyer consoled her. Her parents and Billy's parents came to her side. Everyone believed that she hadn't killed Doctor Bradford. But they didn't understand how she could ever have contemplated such an act. Billy's death had taken a toll on Tinker, both physically and mentally. She hadn't been herself. But taking another person's life? That wasn't something she could have done. They knew that, right?

Tinker grabbed Billy's father's, Mr. Franklin's hand, along with her father's and walked out of the courtroom. The press flooded the courthouse steps. Cameras flashed and reporters thrust microphones into her face. The reporters were getting into her space and throwing various questions at her.

Tinker was scared and angry at the same time. Why couldn't they just leave her alone?

"I have nothing to say," snapped Tinker.

"Why did you do this?" yelled a reporter.

"No questions," said Tinker's father.

They all got into a waiting car. Driving in silence, Tinker felt the need to speak. "I never meant for anyone to go through this," she said with a quivering voice. "Billy was my soul sister. I only cared about her life and the quality of it. Someone was poisoning her."

"How can you be so sure of that?" questioned Billy's father.

"Because the test that she had for cancer was false," Tinker replied. "I had another test done on her. It came back negative. The injections Billy was getting were a deadly virus. Dr. Bradford was giving them to her."

"But why?" questioned Billy's father.

"Greed!" Tinker yelled. "He wanted money for his research lab. Billy was his guinea pig. She thought he was God. Billy believed in him and in what he had said he could do for her. She believed in him so much that she let him use her. Now we realize he altered the results of the tests to make his data look correct. It came out in court," she sobbed.

The car sped up the driveway and stopped in front of an antique, white, plantation-style home with columns. They got out. Tinker turned and wandered away. "I need some time."

It was a crisp autumn day in the Maryland countryside. Tinker wandered among the green, orange, and scarlet fallen leaves. They floated from the trees on the soft breeze and landed on the ground. Whispers between the leaves filled the air. Whispers and mutters. The cold, fresh wind caressed her face. Her curly hair moved ever so in the breeze. Tinker glanced over at the tire swing still hanging on an enormous tree after all these years.

She could hear Billy's laughter filling the air. Billy's long, fiery, orange, curly hair flowed in the wind and those eyes as blue as the summer sky. Tinker wept. How had her life come to this point? From being called 'Oreo' as a child to being called 'a Murderer.' She didn't murder Dr. Bradford. But who did?

Did someone see her slip something into his drink? Follow them to his apartment to watch her struggle to get him inside only to see her scurry out with panic written all over her face? Had there been a third person? Who? Why?

Tinker heard her mother calling from the house to come in for dinner. Her grandmother used to do that when she was a small girl. Her parents named her after her. She was a leading infectious disease specialist. Tinker had followed in her footsteps. She had promised her grandmother when she was just a girl. She even resembled her – the long, raven black hair and dark eyes. Her mother called again.

"Coming, mom!"

She turned and strolled back to the house. Climbing the stairs and taking a deep breath, she opened the door and drifted in. Billy's family filled the house along with her family. The air seemed thick. Oh yes, there was definitely an elephant in the room, and she was it.

"So, what's for dinner?" Tinker asked.

Everyone laughed and then went back to chatting with one another about nothing that made any sense.

"Dinner is served!" called a voice from the dining room.

The families all sat around the table and waited for the blessing. Tinker's father gave a heartfelt one. Then they started passing plates of mouthwatering food around and returned to the mindless chatter.

Tinker excused herself after dinner and went to her childhood bedroom. It had soft, painted pink walls and lace curtains. Her high school trophies still sat on the mantle. Tinker laid down on the soft quilted spread and sobbed. Wiping her tears from her face, she thought of how her life had come to this.

Her mind went backward to the day a phone call from Billy changed their lives forever.

"Tinker, it's Billy. I got my test results back. I have brain cancer," said a frenzied voice on the other end of the line.

"What? How is that possible?" yelled Tinker into the phone.

"My test results. Remember the severe headaches?" sobbed Billy.

"Are you in your lab?" asked Tinker.

"Yes."

"I'll be right there. Don't move."

She could remember how they both hugged each other and cried together. Billy got sick immediately. Tinker was suspicious because Billy was still going to the lab of Dr. Bradford, her lover. Billy and Tinker had argued about him when Billy had first started seeing him. It was known that Dr. Bradford was married and a womanizer. Billy went along with the cheating. They had agreed not to discuss him again to preserve their friendship.

When Billy was admitted to the hospital, Tinker took blood tests on her. No detectable markers for cancer. Billy had the deadly virus that they were working on in Dr. Bradford's lab. He received grant money to find the antidote for the virus. How was any of this possible? Then Tinker remembered the shots that Dr. Bradford had been administering to Billy. Supposedly, vitamin B. By the time Tinker figured this out, Billy had died.

Tears started streaming down her face. She buried her head further into the soft pillows on her bed. The bed felt like it was spiraling. It seemed to move faster and faster. Blackness brought with it an exhausting sleep. She slipped into unconsciousness as exhaustion took its toll on her. Her mind drifted into darkness, and she dreamed. The room felt dull, dark, and cold. It seemed silent, despite the music playing. Tinker stood in Dr. Bradford's office confronting him about Billy.

"You injected her with the deadly virus!" yelled Tinker.

"You're crazy," said Dr. Bradford, trying to stay calm.

"She adored you! She believed in you."

"I did nothing wrong," he said. "I don't even give the injection in the office. One nurse does that."

"You killed her! Now I will kill you!"

"Get out of my office or I'll call security!"

"You'll need more than security when I get through with you," a threatening Tinker replied. "Watch your back!" she yelled as she stormed out.

As she walked out of the doctor's office, a petite, gray-haired woman in a white lab coat was seated at the receptionist desk. She hadn't been there when Tinker came in. She turned to her and said, "Start searching for a new job. This lab will be closed soon."

The woman just smiled.

Tinker got into the elevator and cried. Why had Dr. Bradford injected Billy with that deadly virus? Did he? Or had someone else done it? But why? Billy had thought he loved her and would leave his wife. He lied, and Billy paid the price. He had taken Billy's young life. Soon Tinker would end his. She started working out a strategy. It would require an apology, but the result would be worth it.

Tinker let a few days pass, then called Dr. Bradford. It went right to voicemail.

She left a message. "Daniel, I hope I can call you that. I'm sorry for the way I acted and the things I said. Billy and I were friends for so long. I just couldn't face her death. I would like to make it up to you. Can we meet for dinner?" asked Tinker in a soft, seductive voice. She tried several times before he returned her call.

"How about seven o'clock on Friday night at the Water House Inn?" Daniel asked.

"That would be fantastic." She required the three days to gather the narcotics she would use. Friday came quick, but Tinker had collected everything she would need for the night. She arrived fifteen minutes early to the restaurant so she could find a fairly private table. Tinker ordered a bottle of wine, Billy's favorite, a chardonnay. When Daniel came in, she stood up and embraced him. His posture stiffened. His muscles rigid during her embrace.

"I'm sorry for the way I acted."

He placed his hand on hers. "I understand Billy and you were close," he whispered.

Tinker poured them both a glass of white wine, and they toasted Billy and their new friendship. She tried hard not to let her genuine feelings show. "Stay focused," she thought. She reached into her pocket and touched the pill that would change both their lives.

He couldn't help noticing her nervousness. "Shall we order?" asked Daniel.

His cell phone rang. He glanced at the caller ID. "Please excuse me. I have to take this." Daniel rose from his chair and walked away from the table, dialing a number as he walked out of sight.

"Perfect," thought Tinker. She reached into her pocket, her hand shaking as she fumbled for the pill container. Where is it? Her mind raced. She felt the plastic container in her hand. A sigh of relief came over her. A voice added to her panic.

"Can I get you anything," the tall waiter asked.

"No," Tinker answered.

He walked away. Tinker looked around and took out the pill, slipping it into his glass of wine. It made the wine fizzy. "Stop fizzing," thought Tinker, "or he'll notice." Daniel reappeared.

"Everything all right?" she asked.

He lifted his glass and took a sip and a long glance at her.

"Just fine," he replied.

It didn't take long for Daniel to become ill. His face turned pale. He lay a hand on his stomach and beads of sweat formed on his forehead. Tinker offered to drive him home. She had taken a taxi to the restaurant. He agreed. They paid the check, and the waiter helped her get him into the car. He was unconscious before she left the parking lot.

Daniel lived in a first-floor apartment with a car port near the side door. Tinker struggled with his body, which was dead weight, but she got him into the apartment. She dropped his body onto the large leather couch. Tinker was out of breath and exhausted. Through dim lighting, she saw a picture of Billy on Daniel's yacht on one of the glass side tables. The image brought tears to Tinker's eyes.

She removed Daniel's tie and unbuttoned his shirt. He stirred a little, then moved around, moaning and freaking her out. She waited. He settled down. Tinker continued unbuttoning his shirt. Taking out a syringe from her purse, she removed the end tip. She squirted out some clear liquid, then looked for just the right spot on his chest. His heart would stop. He would then be lifeless.

Her hand trembled as she pricked his pale skin. She paused. Billy's voice filled the room. She looked over at the picture of Billy. Tinker saw the face in the picture frame talking to her.

"Do No Harm! Do No Harm!" the voice kept echoing.

"I can't do this, you bastard!" Tinker yelled at Daniel's body lying on the couch.

She collected everything and marched out the door. Tinker walked several blocks before she hailed a taxicab, just in case anyone had seen her. In fact, someone had. Someone had been watching them all night.

A petite, gray-haired woman placed her gloved hand on Dr. Bradford's doorknob, unlocked it with her key, then entered the apartment. Daniel lay unconscious on the coach. About fifteen minutes later, she left the same way she had slipped in, unnoticed.

Tinker's dark eyes fluttered like a bird landing. She searched around, closing her eyes once more. Sweating, her heart was pounding and her adrenaline was rushing. Tinker wondered whether she dreamt it or not. It was so real, as if she was living it over again. Was her subconscious trying to tell her something? Had she forgotten something significant that had happened that night? She lay on the bed, her eyes closed, examining everything she could remember. Slipping back into darkness, Tinker succumbed to fatigue.

She visualized herself arriving at work early the next morning to dispose of the needle and the remaining drugs. Daniel would wake with a headache and wouldn't remember anything. She'd make up some story, and he'd have to believe it. Daniel deserved that much.

"Damn you, Billy!" Tinker said out loud.

A nurse came in, upset and crying.

"What's the matter?" asked Tinker.

"Dr. Bradford is dead," she said in a quivering voice.

"What?" said Tinker.

"They discovered him dead in his bed this morning," the nurse replied. "The police are investigating right now."

Tinker's world closed in on her. She felt her breath starting to quicken. It was pure panic. An autopsy would reveal the drug she had used at dinner to make him sick. Tinker's fingerprints littered the car and apartment. She had threatened him in his office. The petite, gray-haired woman at the receptionist desk must have overheard everything. Tinker called her father.

"Attorney Wiley's office," said the voice on the other end.

"Hi, Virginia, this is Tinker. Is my dad available?"

"Let me check," she said.

Tinker felt the clock ticking. It seemed to take forever before her father came on the line.

"Tinker, are you alright?" asked her father.

"No," she sobbed.

"What's wrong?"

"I think I may have murdered Dr. Bradford," she replied.

"What?" he shouted into the phone.

"Please come to the hospital right now."

Attorney Wiley left his office. His driver drove him straight to the hospital. It took about an hour in traffic. He went right to Tinker's lab. Two homicide detectives arrived shortly before her father. One was short and the other tall. He recognized them from former cases.

"May I ask what is going on?" said her father.

"Is this a family visit or professional?" asked the tall detective.

"What do you mean?" asked her father.

"Your daughter confessed to giving Dr. Bradford a sedative last night at dinner. Then she drove him back to his apartment and contemplated killing him," replied the detective.

"May I have a few minutes with my daughter alone?"

"We'll be right outside," the shorter detective said with an attitude. They both ambled out the door.

"What the hell is wrong with you?" demanded her father.

Tinker had never seen her father so upset with her. His face reddened and his neck veins were bulging.

"Dad, I didn't kill him. Yes, I thought about it. But Billy's voice told me not to," she said.

"What are you talking about? No one will believe anything so ridiculous as Billy talking to you from her grave. Do you know what I think? You're having a nervous breakdown."

He dialed a number on his phone and spoke to someone. "Yes, we are in her lab," he said.

"You're going to the psychiatric ward," he told Tinker.

"Dad, I'm not crazy!"

"Yes, you are, Tinker," he replied.

Bart Wiley was a tall, dark-skinned man with curly black hair. His looks had a dangerous effect. People either feared him or awed him. He studied his daughter. She looked like a scared little girl. "I'll take care of this," he said with a smile on his face. Turning, he strolled out to speak with the two detectives.

A physician from the psychiatric ward came to the lab. Tinker went with him, as her father had instructed her to do.

Her fingerprints were all over the apartment and over Daniel's car. She had already confessed to part of it. Her attorney argued her grief-stricken state and how it drove her to a breakdown and a psychotic episode. Tinker kept insisting Doctor Bradford was alive when she had left him. Had she dreamed all of this? Maybe her father was right. Maybe she was insane. Bad dreams plagued Tinker all night, waking up repeatedly.

This behavior continued over the next two weeks until it was time to return to the courthouse. Reporters swamped Tinker once more. They filled the courtroom with Billy's, Doctor Bradford's, and Tinker's colleagues. The judge instructed the jury on the sentencing phase. The panel left the courtroom to determine Tinker's fate. The judge allowed her to wait on a bench in a private corridor.

Tinker thought back to the time she and Billy had pulled a prank on their science teacher. They had brought an ice cooler to class with a sign that read, 'Human Head.' They placed the cooler on a lab table with a sign-up list for dissection. The teacher went along with it for a few minutes and then called Billy and Tinker to the front. Tinker laughed to herself. What wonderful memories she had, even with her life in twelve of her "peers" hands.

The side door made a creaking noise. It opened. A petite, grey-haired woman stood there, the one from Dr. Bradford's office, the person the police accused Tinker of making up. She sat down next to her.

Tinker turned her head toward the woman. "Who are you?"

The woman smiled, eyeing Tinker with a vacant expression. Parting her lips, she whispered, "I'm Doctor Bradford's wife, Rosa Paige Bradford."

Tinker trembled. A feeling of imminent danger came over her. She felt her death in the air. Calming herself, she asked, "What do you want?"

Rosa looked into Tinker's eyes. "Revenge, like Billy and Daniel," she said. She raised her hand up and hastened down with a syringe in it. The pain in Tinker's leg took her breath away. Her body weakened.

Mrs. Bradford stood and walked back calmly through the door, unnoticed.

THE VICTORIAN HOUSE

Eva Barnes reached for the switch on her desk lamp. Exhausted from her tedious hours at work and lack of sleep, she was looking forward to the next four days of rest and relaxation. This month had been demanding.

Her mom was hospitalized for her asthma and the rehabilitation center where Eva worked had an increased number of cases. Putting on her coat, wool hat, mitts, and boots she headed toward the parking lot. It had snowed earlier during her work shift. She trudged through the snow to her car and cleared a day's worth of snow off. This bitter March weather had dumped snow every day. She planned on lying down on the couch in front of the fireplace for the next few days.

Eva was a seasoned snow driver. It took her less than fifteen minutes to arrive at home. Coming into the area off the kitchen, she removed her heavy coat and hat. Putting them on the hooks on the wall and then removing her winter boots, she slid her feet into her comfy slippers and took in the quietness of her home.

The kitchen was dark, except for the flashing red light on the answering machine. Eva pushed the message button, noticing the call was from her mom. Panic hit. "Please let it be something simple," thought Eva as she listened to the message.

"Eva, please call me right away. Something serious has happened!" replied her mother.

She dialed her number, hands trembling. "Mom, what happened?"

"Abigail died," her mother said.

Eva didn't respond. She detested that woman who had ruined their lives.

"Your stepmother," her mother responded.

"That's too bad, but why would I care? I haven't seen or heard from my dad or her in forty years," snapped Eva.

"Your sister is at his house."

"I'm not going, mom. Love you, good night."

Eva stood there silent for several minutes, then tears slipped from her eyes. Forty years of anguish and sadness flowed forth. Her pencil-thin frame shook and her sobs sounded like an injured animal. Could she let this man into her life? He had abandoned her sister and her. But worst of all he abandoned her mother.

Sarah Cowley was thirteens year old and Eva was eight years old when their dad had left. He had divorced their mother and married their mother's best friend. Eva sat down and thought about Sarah, her sister. She was Eva's rock and had helped her mother take care of her.

She dialed Sarah's cell number.

"Hello, it's Sarah."

"Hi, it's me."

"Eva! Are you coming? Please!" pleaded Sarah.

"I don't know, Sarah. Let me sleep on it. I'll let you know in the morning."

Could Eva let her sister handle her stepmother's death alone? Was she that bitter and full of hate? Eva went, even if she didn't want to. Leaving at five the next morning, she set the GPS for 10 Howard St., Kittery, Maine. How was she able to recall that address after all these years? It was a home she had treasured as a young girl, one with elegant antiques and dogs.

Eva snapped herself back to reality and drove. As she rode, her mind wandered to her dad. When she was little, they would drive to Maine and sing in the car. She loved him then, but now her feelings were suspended in time.

Speeding up the long driveway three hours later, she paused halfway up and looked at the huge Victorian. It reminded her of a giant monster that might devour her alive. She wanted to turn back, but then she saw Sarah waving at her. Eva continued up into the monster's clutches.

"Thanks for coming," said Sarah. "Weird things are going on here. Dad tells me one version and Helen, the caregiver, tells me another about how Abigail died. You don't know who to believe. Helen is like a buzzard circling around dad for Abigail's money."

Eva stepped back, peering into her sister's emerald green eyes. "I hope Helen the buzzard pecks him to death. Forty damn years, Sarah. My childhood and most of all, our mom's health. Forgotten birthdays and holidays, not even a card. I will give him and the others two days, then I'm leaving. I don't care if they murdered Abigail."

Her sister looked stunned.

Eva didn't care. She needed to get this over with and go back to her life.

"Eva," Sarah whispered. "No one in this entire town, not even Dad's lawyer, realized he had children. We are his best-kept secret." They glanced at each other, smiled, and started giggling.

Eva said, "Even Dad forgot about us."

"No," Sarah answered, "that's not true. He asked about you last night because I mentioned you might not be coming."

"I came here for you, not him. I feel nothing but disgust for him. I don't want him in my life," replied Eva.

They both entered the Victorian. It still looked like something out of an antique magazine. Standing in the sunlit kitchen was a tattered, old grey-haired man. Eva couldn't believe her eyes. "Is this my father?" she thought. As he spoke, she recognized his voice.

"Eva, you came. It makes me happy. My Abigail died right here in this kitchen. I can't believe it. One minute she was speaking, then she collapsed on the table."

"Maybe someone poisoned her," Eva said.

Sarah shot her a nasty look.

"No, they said it was her heart," he responded.

Eva thought, "That's impossible. Abigail didn't have a heart and, if she did, it was made of stone."

The kitchen door flew open, and a small silvery-haired woman strolled in.

"This must be the buzzard," Eva thought.

Helen extended her hand to greet Eva. As their hands touched, the hair on Eva's neck stood straight up. She felt evil in the woman's touch.

"I'm Helen, your father and stepmother's caregiver."

"I'm Eva, the other daughter."

"I understood you weren't coming," said Helen.

"Does it matter?" answered Eva.

Helen glared at her. It made Eva bristle.

"I've taken care of both of them for years. I'm here to make certain your father is alright," Helen snapped.

Eva excused herself and went into the living room to wait until they left for the church service.

The service was uncomfortable for the stepdaughters. People were whispering and pointing at them. The minister kept going on and on about what an amazing woman Abigail was and all she had carried out for the community. It made Eva sick to her stomach. The coffee hour after wasn't much better. The members of the congregation gathered around them, asking questions they didn't want to deal with. They were glad to get back to the house. Tired, their father went to rest.

Sarah wanted to show Eva what she had discovered in the checkbooks. There were glaring inconsistencies. Helen had been stealing for years.

"Who cares," responded Eva

"I demand to know how Abigail died and where," Sarah said.

"Here's the answer." Eva handed Sarah the bills from the hospital, along with a death certificate. Cause of Death: heart failure.

"I don't believe she died of heart failure. I think Helen had something to do with her death," said Sarah.

"Why?" answered Eva.

Just then an awful groaning came from their father's room. Both women jumped up and rushed to see what was going on. Their father was rolling around on the bed in agonizing pain.

"Dad, what's wrong?" shouted Sarah.

Eva noticed a bottle on the nightstand. She read the label. It was Abigail's sulfur pills. Eva remembered her father was allergic to sulfur. Why would he have taken them?

"Dad, dad!" He couldn't answer. He was lifeless.

Sarah was holding him in her arms, tears flowing down her face.

Sarah sobbed. "Call 911!"

They both stared at their father. In the distance, they heard sirens coming closer and closer.

The next morning, their father's lawyer, Attorney Gilmore, showed up. They both had swollen eyes and black circles. They hadn't slept at all.

"I'm here this morning to read you a letter I received from your father," he said. "Shall I read it?"

They nodded their heads yes.

"To Whom It May Concern: I, Harry White, took my wife Abigail's life on March 4th with poison. I did this because she planned to divorce me and leave me penniless. I couldn't betray my daughters again. They are to inherit my estate."

Eva and Sarah sat there in silence, staring at Mr. Gilmore.

Sarah spoke up first. "Are you sure he wrote that letter, and not someone else?"

"It's his handwriting," replied the lawyer. "After reviewing a few details with the law enforcement, you two will be wealthy women."

Eva started laughing.

"Stop that!" yelled Sarah.

Eva laughed, then said, "This is how he makes up for forty years? Well, I would say it's one hell of an apology." She kept laughing.

Sarah wept.

THE INHERITANCE

===

Two black limousines simultaneously pulled into a cobble-stone driveway of a grand mansion. The cream color of the paint shone. They secured the wooden shutters. Twisted fencing kept the estate encircled, while trimmed hedges surrounded it. The drivers got out, opened the doors, and two women emerged from the vehicles. One was worldly looking, even sophisticated for her young twenty-something age. The other was disheveled, her hair bleached beyond any recognizable color. Her clothes looked like she had slept in them for many days. She lit a cigarette. Her hands trembled as she dragged on it with force to fill her lungs rapidly. Life hadn't been favorable to her for twenty-some years. Yet both women thought to themselves, "Do I know you?"

"I'm Camille Atwood," the well-dressed young woman responded, extending her small manicured hand.

The other woman put out her cigarette, flipping it onto the well-kept lawn.

"Jazz Just Jazz," she said. "Do you think this is for real? I could use a few extra bucks."

"You look like you're doing great," Camille smiled.

The heavy wooden door of the estate made a squeaking noise, surprising both of them. A middle-aged, silver-haired woman in a gray maid's uniform called to them. "Don't just stand in the entrance, come in. Your accommodations are ready!"

The drivers took the women's travel bags and walked into the house.

"Come along!" barked the woman. "You must get settled before we serve dinner. It is 7:00 o'clock sharp. Jazz, wear something more proper. And no smoking." She turned and hastened away through a door. The two women stood alone in the tiled foyer.

"What does she mean more proper?" asked Jazz.

"I think she means your jeans. The holes and skin are a bit much for dinner attire. No sweatshirt either," answered Camille.

"You'd think she was my grandma telling me what to wear," Jazz said.

"This way," a man's voice called. It was the driver beckoning them to the second floor. A luxurious mahogany staircase with sturdy rails led up to the next level. It curved in such a manner that the delightful surprise of their names on the doors of their rooms was hidden.

"This is creepy," said Jazz.

"I know," replied Camille, rolling her sky-blue eyes.

Camille turned the doorknob and entered her candlelit room. She felt along the ice-cold surface for a light switch. She couldn't believe the décor when the lights lit up the place. They covered the walls in framed pictures of her at various stages of her life, from nursery school to college, including her failures and accomplishments. She took a deep breath and turned around to hear the metallic click of the door locking. A shock of fear ripped through her whole body. Camille turned the doorknob. It wouldn't open. She tugged on it with considerable force.

A voice crackled through the air vent in the wall. "Dinner at seven!"

Camille yanked her shoe off and flung it with force at the air-vent. "Damn you! Whoever you are, I am not hungry." She reached into the pocket of her sweater vest. The ivory grip of her forty-five felt cold against her hand as she sat on the edge of the bed. That's when she saw the picture on the nightstand.

It appeared to be an ultrasound of a baby. The word "twins" was scribbled on a piece of paper attached to the frame. Was Jazz her twin? Is that what the intimate feeling was? Did she have a sister? Was that her inheritance?

Camille got up and headed toward the door, then paused. Something or someone scratching at the door alerted her. What was it?

"Please let me in, I'm scared!" sighed a childish voice. Camille turned the doorknob with force and yanked open the door, gripping her hand on the revolver in her vest pocket and her other side bracing herself. It was Jazz. Camille saw the terror on her face. Jazz was crimson and blotchy, her eyelids puffy.

"Can I come in to your room? Mine is a horror show," Jazz said with a cracking voice.

"Mine isn't much better," said Camille.

"Dinner is served," a familiar female voice said.

"Shut up!" yelled Jazz, putting her hands to her ears. Her voice was something between a sob and a shout. She clawed at her arms as if she had poison ivy.

Jazz was frail. Her blue eyes stared listlessly, dull, and lifeless. Her skin was pale. Camille had known many drug users in recovery that acted like Jazz. She scratched her arms, picked at scabs on her face, and her hands had a constant shake. Camille was the assistant district attorney in Chicago. She prosecuted many junkies. She knew how to take care of herself. Her curly blonde hair and petite size often confused people. But Jazz was a victim and a recovering addict.

"No!" yelled Camille. "We're leaving."

"No transportation to town until tomorrow. Dinner is served."

A male voice called up to them, "Come downstairs and allow me to introduce myself, ladies!"

The women eyed each other, then walked out of the room and over to the staircase. They stared down at him.

"I'm Brock Erickson, your half-brother," he said with little or no emotion.

Camille and Jazz stared at him, each other, and then back at him.

"Please come down and have dinner."

Camille gently took Jazz's hand and walked down the staircase into the dining room. She hoped it was the correct decision. They didn't know how many people were in the house. The dining room was formal, with a selection of food set for a king… or perhaps their last supper? Jazz and Camille sat on either side of the dinner table with Brock at the head. Jazz ate like she hadn't had an adequate meal in days. Camille ate very little, not trusting anything in this house. She wanted to protect them from harm until the morning. Camille couldn't care less about the inheritance now.

Brock said, "Camille, why don't you tell us about yourself. You're the counselor."

Jazz pushed back her chair, slamming down her fist on the table. "You're a damn lawyer? I detest lawyers. They've screwed me my whole life. From foster care to prison." She sweated profusely and dabbed her face with the cloth napkin.

"I assure you, Jazz, I am not that kind of lawyer," Camille said. "He is just trying to pit us against each other. Aren't you, Brock?"

"That's what they all say!" yelled Jazz. "Do you realize what happens to junkies?" She caught herself and took a deep breath, then sat down and became quiet. All she wanted now was that one element that would make her feel better. But she knew she must resist the power that was trying to take over and rule her existence.

"You should go first, Brock," said Camille. "You invited us here and decorated our rooms so nicely."

His narrow face had a slight grin. His deep brown, piercing eyes twinkled like he had evil on his mind. "I'm glad you like the décor in your rooms. I discovered all the items in my father's safe. He must have had someone watching you two for your entire lives. I can't get my inheritance until you get yours. I want mine. So that's why you're here," Brock said.

"Who is our mother?" asked Camille.

Brock hesitated as if channeling an evil spirit. "My father, your mother's professor, got her pregnant. She was one of his pupils. Yes, Jazz, believe it or not, your mother, at one time, was intelligent. She wanted to keep both of you bitches. My father wouldn't hear of it. This wasn't the first time it happened… the pregnancies. But it was the first time someone wanted to keep them. I was away at college, and my mother was bedridden. You were taken at birth and given away to an agency to find good homes." Brock took a deep breath as if it bored him.

"Well, that didn't happen," said Jazz.

"What happened to our mother?" Camille demanded.

"She went into a deep postpartum depression and tried to poison my parents," Brock said. "Your mother was Ester Clare. That was her name. She was institutionalized and never recovered from the loss of you two." He drew a long breath again. "She committed suicide."

"Damn it, Brock. Why did it take so long for you to contact us?" asked Camille.

"Because I would never reach out to either of you," he said. "But my damn father left a clause in his will for you two when you reached thirty. I believe your birthdays are next week. You both will inherit a generous sum of money," he said in a disgusted tone.

"We will get money?" asked Jazz. "Real money?"

"Yes, and you can buy all the dope you want, Jazz," he snarled.

"Don't talk to my sister like that," said Camille. "Jazz hasn't had the same opportunities we have. You and your father should have helped her long before this. You probably hoped she overdosed and died."

"Yes, I did! I also hoped a person you prosecuted would kill you," he said.

"Well, Brock, it sounds that your wishes didn't come true. Here we are. Tomorrow you will have to provide us some of your father's money," laughed Camille.

"Let's go to bed, Jazz," said Camille. The women placed their hands around each other's shoulders and walked out of the dining room and up the stairs.

"Can I sleep with you?" begged Jazz. I'm scared we will die

"We will not die," Camille assured her.

Camille opened the door. They were surprised. The room was cheerful and inviting, and all the picture frames had disappeared. The only one left behind was that of the twins.

"Looks like someone wants us to be comfortable in our room," said Camille. "Do you need something to sleep in, Jazz?"

"No, I prefer to sleep in my clothes. When you live the way I do, you sleep in your clothes most of the time. I'm sorry about my outburst at dinner. I've had such a dreadful life and only been clean for a short while."

"You're not going back to that lifestyle, Jazz. I will take care of you, no matter how much money we get tomorrow. We have a lot of time to make up for."

"How do you plan to protect us until we get out of here?" asked Jazz.

Camille put her hand into her vest pocket and pulled out her revolver. She laid it in on the nightstand next to the bed.

"I'm a decent shot," said Camille.

The women lay in the dark next to each other. Camille put her hand on Jazz's hand.

"There has always been something missing in my life. Now I know it was you. I don't care about the inheritance. You're my inheritance," whispered Camille.

Tears rolled down Jazz's face. For the first time in her life, she felt protected. She had never known genuine affection. Now she had a sister. Now she had a chance at a different life. Jazz squeezed Camille's hand. They fell asleep, holding each other's hand.

Camille woke up early and dressed. Jazz woke with the jitters, her body itching. She dug her nails into her arms, causing them to bleed. It was unpleasant for Camille to watch. She tried calming her down and cleaned up her arms.

Jazz jumped up and darted for the door. "Let's get our money and leave!" she yelled to Camille.

Camille stopped packing her bags and followed Jazz. She didn't want her sister downstairs alone. Camille still didn't know how many people were in the house. Someone had changed the décor in their rooms last night while they all had dinner. For all she knew, there could be secret panels in the mansion.

Brock was in the study and called to them as they came down the staircase.

"Did you sleep well?" he asked.

"Do you care?" snapped Jazz, still dazed by the early morning wake-up.

Camille interrupted them. "Let's get busy with this paperwork so we can leave."

"That's what I like about you, all business." Brock took two folders out of the drawer of his antique desk. He handed each of them an envelope, explaining the details. He left copies for them to read and sign. He closed the pocket doors behind him.

"Do you still want me to come with you?" asked Jazz.

"Of course," replied Camille. "This money will help with your recovery. Then we can travel and get to know each other. Even if I am a lawyer." They both laughed.

A hissing came through the air vent, followed by a dense mist of rolling death.

"He is gassing us," sobbed Jazz.

A voice from the wall air vent cackled. "Now, I don't have to share anything with you two."

Camille and Jazz started coughing, their eyes stinging. Jazz pulled Camille to the floor.

"We can breathe better down here," said Jazz.

"How did Jazz know that?" Camille thought as she reached inside her vest pocket. Sheer panic washed over her. Her gun was on the nightstand stand. The damn nightstand! In the confusion of helping Jazz, she had forgotten all about it. Camille glanced toward Jazz. Jazz knew they were in trouble.

As they lay on the floor, coughing and choking, they heard shouting from outside the door. Two shots rang out. Then the doors opened to bring them life-saving air. The women were on the floor, hugging each other.

Camille stood up first. She stumbled to the open door. On the tile foyer lay Brock. Over him loomed Ethel, the housekeeper, Camille's gun in her hand.

"Put the gun down," said Camille as calmly as she could.

Ethel did as Camille asked.

"Why?" Camille questioned.

"I am your grandmother," replied Ethel.

THE LETHAL LESSON

It was a raw, wet night. The wind blew icy crystals against the house for what seemed like hours. The heat blasted, but it still seemed cool. London Kennedy settled in her bed covered with wool blankets and dressed in flannel pajamas. She felt her consciousness fading away and her thoughts ending. "No dreaming tonight," London whispered, slipping into unconsciousness. Her breathing slowed, and she escaped into sleep.

Elijah Becker, her pupil, stood in front of her, his black tattooed arms at his side. He turned to London. "You're dead, you squealer!" he hissed at her. He turned to the class. "Remember what she did."

London woke to a humming sound, like bees. She shot straight up in her bed, covered in perspiration and panting. She glanced around to gain a sense of where she was. The dream was a recurring nightmare every night of her week-long February school vacation.

Today, London Kennedy would have to face her class. Elijah wouldn't be there. They expelled him from school and arrested him for the drugs found in his locker. His locker was searched before they removed him from London's classroom. They had found many types of drugs and paraphernalia. He also was a known gang leader. Elijah had a lengthy record, as did many of London's students. Her father, a former police chief, begged her not to take the job. Cedar High School had several gangs and drug problems.

Most of the classrooms were bursting at the seams, leaving slower learners behind. London struggled to give her students examples and connect with them. It was an impossible task. Her students lived below the poverty level, so there were many drop-outs. It seemed to London that the only chance for her students to get out of their condition was to join gangs.

London reflected on when she took this teaching position. She wasn't certain she'd like high school, being thirty and youthful looking. She was small with a slim body. Her large piercing green eyes complemented her chestnut hair and pale skin. The boys would often flirt with her at school. Now, in the student's eyes, she was a squealer… and a mark.

Getting out of bed, she shuffled to the kitchen to pour herself a cup of coffee. Thank goodness for timers on coffee makers. She opened the back door and stepped out onto the ice-covered deck. It had been a much-needed vacation from school. Steam was coming from her coffee cup as she wrapped her hands around the cup to enjoy the warmth. She was wrapped in a bathrobe and warm slippers. The sunlight was peeking out of the horizon. Its brilliant rays showed through the woods. The trees swayed, casting off the light snow clinging to every brittle branch. The chill caught everything in its embrace.

London felt uneasy, alert. She scanned around, searching for eyes she sensed might be watching her. London drew a few calming breaths. "This is silly," she thought, as she sipped her coffee and gazed over the woods. She could protect herself. Being the daughter of a retired police chief had its advantages. She remembered the times she spent at the shooting range with her dad. Her father wanted her to be a police officer, but she became a teacher. She took criminal justice courses but realized that teaching was her passion. Now her classroom made her appear more like a prison warden. She despised it.

London looked from the deck at her car in the driveway. She packed her car with her material for school. Now all she needed to do was to get dressed. Creaking noises in the adjoining wooded area startled her, along with a bright light flickering back-and-forth in the trees. It must be a reflection and the sound of an animal walking on the crunching snow, she thought. London turned back to go into the house, her long, hair blowing ever so slightly in the wind.

As London dressed, she thought about her student Elijah. He yelled profanities at her in the classroom as he was being taken away by the police. Elijah knew it was London who reported him. It relieved her that he wouldn't be in school for the rest of the year. They found no weapons in the school, but in her heart, she knew they were stashed there some place. It was just a matter of time before someone used them.

London finished getting ready and gathered up her purse and coat. Starting down the stairs, she gripped the handrail until she reached the last step and dashed to her car in the driveway. The car was warm and ready to go, as London had started it before getting dressed. Once again, she heard snow crunching and saw the wavy reflection in the air. The twinkling light moved through the woods back-and-forth. "What is that light?" she thought.

A black silhouette of a person stepped from behind the trees and stood at the end of her long driveway. The figure was garbed in dark clothing, and a hood covered its face. There was some reflection coming from the garment. She could sense hostile eyes peering at her. The silhouette moved its head, and the twinkling light appeared. It must be some company name on the hooded shirt. That was the moving light London had seen in the woods. She felt alone and isolated. London lived on a country road where the houses were far apart and few streetlights. The figure never took their eyes off her. This sent a chill up her spine. This was no casual visitor or someone out for a morning walk.

"Do you need help?" London called out.

No answer.

London inched toward her car. The figure started sprinting up the long driveway as if it was beginning a race. Fumbling with her keys, she dropped them on the ground. Her mind raced as she scooped them up and pressed the door opener on the key ring. London hurled herself into the front seat and locked the door. The clicking noise of the lock sounded like a revolver's trigger being pulled back.

The black figure started pounding on the car window. Her breathing quickened. She felt prickling hairs on the back of her neck. London was shivering. She was trapped in her own car in her own driveway. She tried to clear her choppy mind. Without a thought, London put her foot on the accelerator. The engine revved. Why didn't it move? She realized she hadn't put the car in gear. The figure held tight to the car door handle. London put the vehicle in reverse and accelerated. The person hastened down the driveway. Who was this person? Why had they not communicated?

She put her foot on the brake. Drawing a deep breath, trying to calm herself, her hand tumbled as she reached over and patted the side pocket of her purse. London looked into the backup camera in the car, and the figure was once again stalking toward the vehicle. Panicked, she released her foot from the brake and backed-up again. The person stopped and stood in the middle of the driveway like they were figuring out what she would do next. Its hand reached up, pulling the hood off its head. In the natural light of the day, London could see it was Elijah. His golden-brown skin, thick-curly brown hair, and his muscular build was a frightening sight.

She was astounded. London threw the car into park. She opened the door and jumped out.

"What do you want?" she demanded.

"You know damn well what I want, you bitch. I got arrested and expelled from school. I won't graduate now because of you!" he yelled.

"That's your fault. You're the one who was peddling drugs in school and the leader of a gang. Again, what are you doing in my driveway?"

"I'm here to show you what happens to people who squeal."

"Leave now, Elijah, while you have a chance. Or I'll call the police, and you'll be in more trouble."

"Trouble? You don't know what trouble is. I'm here to teach you a lesson."

London put her hand in the side pocket of her purse and pulled out her small revolver. She pointed it straight at him. Her father's voice sounded in her head. Never point a gun, unless you're sure you will use it, or you could get hurt.

"Leave, or I'll use it!" London yelled.

Elijah laughed. "You? I don't think so. You're in my classroom now, teach."

"Where are your gang members?" London asked.

"Don't need them." He took out his cell phone. "All I have to do is push a button, and my boys will be here."

"All I have to do is pull the trigger, and your boys will find you dead," replied London.

The words echoed in her head. Could she shoot one of her students? When her principal, Alice Davenport, asked her that question in school, she hadn't hesitated to say, "Yes." London was one of the armed teachers at the high school. Now, with Elijah standing in front of her, in her driveway, she wasn't sure she could pull the trigger. Was his life less valuable than hers? He was just a teenager, with so much life left. London's adrenaline spiked.

Elijah moved. London warned him again. She saw him reach behind his back. He seemed to freeze for a second. There it was. A gun. Had he come to kill her? Was she going to die?

"Put the gun down!" she yelled.

He laughed as he squeezed the trigger of the gun. London knew what the click sound was. Pop! The sound of the weapon echoed through the woods. The force of the bullet pushed her to the ground. The pain in her arm burned like hot charcoals embedded under her skin. A stream of red liquid flowed from her wound. Everything went silent. London could feel her pulse pounding through her body. At that moment she felt no pain, no sorrow, just silence. "Someone has shot me. I'm dead." She just lay there. Elijah moved closer.

London felt the gun in her hand. "Wait," she thought. He turned like he was leaving. Maybe he thought she was dead. She lay still and tried not to breathe. Elijah moved toward her again. London's adrenaline helped her move swiftly to her knees. The marksmen did what her father trained her to do. Pop, pop! Again, the sound of two gunshots rang out through the woods. She knew just where to fire. It knocked Elijah back a foot or two, and he fell. Blood poured down his shirt as he hit the ground. A red pool formed underneath him. Tears rolled down London's pale skin face. Remember, said her father, shoot to kill.

THE DEATH NOTICE

Adam Chambers heard the ticking of the clock on the wall and the intimidating sounds of the machines surrounding him. The dull white hospital walls seemed to close in on him. These walls told stories of shattered souls and unfulfilled dreams. Doctors and nurses strolled in and out. The hospital bed linens were scratchy and uncomfortable. The shuffling of feet on the floor got Adam's groggy attention. Sitting in an armchair across from him was his charming wife, Audrey, staring into space. He tried sitting up but sank back on the pillow.

"Audrey," Adam said with a hoarse tone, his throat sore from the tubes used during his five-hour cancer surgery.

She smiled, her blue eyes sparkling. "It sounds like the surgeon got all the cancer. In fact, ninety-nine-point-five percent, he claims. But just in case, you'll need a few rounds of chemotherapy."

Chemo started a month after Adam's surgery. He had several rounds of treatment over the next three years with several remissions. His last treatment was in May, and he passed away in July. Adam died the day after their 30th wedding anniversary. He had promised he would make it to her birthday and their anniversary. Adam never broke a promise. Audrey had held him in her arms as he took his last breath.

"I love you. Don't cry," he said. Then he was gone.

The day of Adam's funeral, a soldier dressed in his Air Force uniform had stood in front of the Chambers family and their friends and said, "On behalf of the President of the United States, the Department of the Air Force, and a grateful nation, we offer this flag for the faithful and dedicated service of Master Sergeant Adam Chambers."

Those words played over and over in Audrey Chambers' head. Her fingers traced the display case she had placed the flag in. A flag that would never be opened or flown again.

Now, three months later, Audrey had completed the estate work. She was glad for the quiet in her home. Things had settled down. Probate was completed, and all the retirements were notified, or so she thought. Grief, she had learned, was a love that you wanted to give but couldn't. It gathered in the hallowed part of her chest. Her life as she had known it was gone. All that was left was darkness.

Silence covered her once noisy home. Audrey's face showed distress as she closed her blue eyes, tears running down her pale ivory skin. She wiped her red and swollen eyes. She looked around, her was vision blurry. It was difficult to see. She missed her husband.

The family dog, Harley, started barking at his arch-enemy, the mailman. That startled Audrey. She gathered up the mail and went back into the house. Junk mail, most of it addressed to Adam. Would his mail ever stop?

One letter caught her eye. It was from one of Adam's retirement benefits. Opening and reading it, she sat down in shock.

"Dear Audrey Chambers. We have been notified that you are deceased. Therefore, your husband's retirement benefits have been suspended."

Audrey started laughing and put the letter down. "This has to be a scam or a joke," she thought. Who sends a person a letter if they're presumed dead? It should have been addressed to her estate. It gave her thirty days to respond.

"I'll play," she thought. Audrey dialed one number on the letter. After a parade of voice prompts, she spoke with an actual person. Audrey explained the situation, and that she was alive. The voice on the other end promised to straighten out the account and get back to her in a few days.

Audrey ran her fingers through her chestnut locks. "I need a haircut," she thought. "Maybe I'll get one tomorrow." It was early, but she tired. She lifted Harley, and they went to bed.

That morning she composed a response to her death notice. She sent a copy of the letter to the consumer's fraud protection in the state, and the law enforcement in her town. This had to be a scam.

Several weeks passed, and Audrey received a call from Police Chief Ashford. He was curious about the letter and why she thought it was a scam. She explained it was a deceitful way to defraud spouses out of their inheritance. It was such a slight amount of money that people might not notice, and it would make the retirement company seem more profitable.

"But how?" he asked.

"Think about it. If one hundred people didn't get this insignificant amount, it would add up," Audrey explained.

"Good thinking," he said. "I'll contact them and see what's going on."

Later that day, Audrey received a call from Eva Cole, a state consumer protection investigator. She, too, questioned why Audrey thought this was a scam. Once again, Audrey explained what she thought. Eva agreed it was a theory to think about.

The phone rang again. "Hello," Audrey said.

"I am Chandler Crawford, the head of the investment company," the voice on the other end said. "I'm wondering why you have involved other people in this mistake?"

"I don't think it is a mistake," said Audrey.

"Madam, I can assure you, we have dealt with it," he replied.

"Then we have nothing else to discuss," replied Audrey and hung up.

When her bank statement arrived a month later, Audrey noticed the investment company had taken money from her husband's retirement account. She was furious, grabbed the statement and drove straight to the bank.

The bank manager was astonished and called the company. She informed them that Audrey was seated in front of her and alive. The person on the other end asked to speak with Audrey.

"Hello Mrs. Chambers, I am Martha Field," said the voice with a distinct southern drawl. "They have assigned me to your claim. I will need the following paperwork from you: your husband's death certificate, a copy of your driver's license, and your marriage license."

"Why?" asked Audrey.

"That's how this works," Maratha said.

"No!" Audrey said. She had had enough. "If I don't get an answer by the end of the day, there will be dire consequences for all involved." She hung up and thanked the bank person and drove home.

As Audrey pulled into her driveway, she noticed a blue car parked across the street. It had been there when she left for the bank. She snapped a picture on her phone of its license plate. She thought, "What about all those phone hang-ups?" Was she being watched? Had she discovered an enormous investment company was cheating people? She shivered, frightened.

Pulling out of her driveway, she headed for the police station. The blue car followed behind her. The windows were tinted so Audrey could not see who was driving. "I'll lose him," she thought. She drove around all the side streets by her house until she couldn't see the car anymore. Pulling into the police station parking lot, she scanned one more time to see if the vehicle was anywhere around. Audrey asked to see Chief Ashford.

Chief Ashford was a gray-haired man with brownish skin. He had a kindness about him. "Mrs. Chambers, please have a seat and tell me what I can do for your today," he said.

Audrey sat down and took a deep breath. "Well, for starters my apprehensions about the investment company, the blue car parked in front of my house, and the phone hang-ups." Audrey told Chief Ashford everything that had been going on since the last time they spoke.

"I thought I had worked out the issue after my conversation with the company," he said. He had found Audrey's story a little far-fetched. But the blue car caught his interest, since Audrey had taken a picture of the license plate number.

"Let me run the plates," he said.

It took a brief time for the chief to run the plates and notify the owner. It was a rental company at the airport. The name on the rental agreement was Adam Chambers.

"That's impossible!" said Audrey. She cried. "What's going on?"

"I don't know," the chief said. "Looks like you may have uncovered a scam. I'm worried you may be in danger."

Audrey was fearless. She had faced her husband's illness and taken care of him until he died in her arms. That company wouldn't steal her money, scare her, or cheat anyone else.

"I'll assign undercover police to watch your home," said the chief.

"I want to help," said Audrey.

"Do you own a firearm?" he asked.

"Yes," she replied.

"Will you use it?" he asked.

"If I have to. I've never fired it at a person."

"We'll watch you as close as we can, but something could happen," he replied.

"Then I'll use it," Audrey replied.

When Audrey returned home, the blue car was gone. Maybe they were riding around trying to find her. As she opened the door, it surprised her that Harley hadn't come to greet her. He always did. Audrey noticed a potent smell of aftershave hanging in the air. Panic set in. Her heart beat rapid as Harley entered the room. He had a hard time standing. Had someone drugged him? She comforted him, then walked through the house to see if anyone was still there. What would she do if people were there? "Stop thinking like that," she told herself. They were looking for something, not trying to hurt her. She hoped that was true.

There was no doubt in her mind that someone had been in her home. Audrey realized she had failed to arm the house alarm. She moved deliberately up the stairs to the other rooms. She went to the closet in her bedroom and opened the safe. Audrey took out her revolver and loaded it. This piece of cold metal would now be her best friend.

"Damn you, Adam, for leaving me," Audrey said out loud.

Every time she heard a sound, she would touch her weapon. "This is nonsense, and I will not live like this." Audrey gathered up Harley, set the alarm, and went to bed. She had little sleep that night.

The next morning, she checked the surveillance cameras. Audrey saw someone wandering around the property. The image was dressed in a dark hooded sweatshirt and pants. "Who was this?" she thought. Maybe she should call the police? First, she needed to get dressed. To complete her outfit for the day, Audrey slipped on her concealed weapons vest. The vest looked like an ordinary piece of clothing. She could carry her weapon without an extra holster and remain concealed. It provided easy access to her new best friend. Gun in place, she started her day.

Checking her text messages, she found one from Chief Ashford. It said that one of his officers had been walking around her property last night. It relieved Audrey that it had been the police. She texted back that she had gotten her gun and thought someone had entered her house when she was gone because of the aftershave smell and Harley's odd behavior. He texted back that he was on his way. He made it in record time.

"After you left yesterday, I called the investment company, and they assured me it had been a genuine mistake declaring you deceased. The company told me that Social Security had informed one of their employees you had passed away in June 1989. But after she had contacted them, they realized it was another Audrey Chambers. They hoped they had cleared the situation up," he said.

"That is untrue," said Audrey. "I checked with Social Security since the investment company told me the same story. There was no one named Audrey Chambers who died on that date. I also checked the mobile app. How many of me are there? The answer came back: two. We're both alive."

"I've got to take them at their word. My hands are tied," the chief said.

"What about the aftershave smell and Harley being drugged?" Audrey said with anger in her voice.

"I will keep the police on duty at your house for a few more days. The company has promised me this is over, and they would take care of it."

"They think I'm a crazy old lady," said Audrey. "I'm not. And they better keep their word, or they will see themselves on the evening broadcast."

The chief laughed and excused himself. "I'll check back in a few days," he said.

Audrey thanked him and went about her day. Every time she left the house, she would set the alarm.

Adam, her husband, had been in special forces in the Air Force, and that is when Audrey learned to use a gun. She went to the firing range many times with him. But she had never fired it at a person. Now she was furious, and she wouldn't let this company frighten her.

She could see Adam rolling his eyes and saying, "Why all this fuss over $84.96. It's not like you need it."

But he had earned it, and that was the entire purpose of this. Besides that, she was positive she had uncovered something that the investment company didn't want public.

The doorbell rang, causing Harley to bark. Audrey could see a man with a bouquet at the door. No florist truck in the driveway or on the street. Where had he come from? Had he come to hurt her? Was this her poison apple? She tapped her vest and then opened the door.

"Audrey Chambers?" he asked.

Audrey hesitated. What if she said no? Would he go away? Then she sniffed the potent odor of his aftershave. He had been the one in her house and drugged Harley. This was the intruder. "What to do?" she thought.

"Yes," she replied, noticing a card protruding from the funeral type floral arrangement. Audrey grabbed it. Her hands surprised the man. She snapped the envelope from the floral arrangement.

She tore open the envelope and read the card out loud. "The next time these will be your funeral flowers. Stop investigating."

The man was so stunned and frozen to the steps.

Stepping back and reaching into her vest, she drew her weapon. She pointed her pearl-handled gun at him.

"I want long stem roses to be my funeral flowers. Tell that to whoever sent you! Never enter my home again." Audrey said. Cocking the gun.

THE RAT TRAIL

The blare of the Block Island Ferry horn caught her attention as it glided out into the Thames River. No need for a clock, the ship leaves promptly at 7:00 AM. Another springtime day teased summer to come forward. Flowers and trees showed off their buds, birds sang in harmony, and squirrels scampered up a pole that held the bird feeder full of seeds. Virginia Adams, known by Ginny, saw this scene every morning while sipping her first mug of coffee.

Ginny's two dogs barked at the squirrels and birds in the backyard. She noticed there was another animal now playing with the others. It was 'Chip,' the chipmunk. He was a tiny, round little creature with white-and-black stripes running down his back. Chip scurried back and forth to the shed. Ginny smiled to herself. Her summer friend had come back. She noted that he looked chunkier, and his tail looked different. She realized it was a different chipmunk every year, but she pretended it was the same.

Ginny went inside to make another cup of coffee. The screen door opened, and Ivy, her daughter, appeared in the kitchen. "Some coffee?" asked Ginny.

"Sure," responded Ivy.

The women moved back outside to enjoy their coffee and the sights and sounds. Ginny had piled her brownish hair onto her head with a colorful hair clip. Her blue eyes sparkled in the sunlight. Ivy resembled her mom, except for her grayish eyes. Ginny was a retired nurse with a medium build, and Ivy was an educator and petite. They both enjoyed doing the same things and spending time together.

Chip darted to the birdfeeder and back underneath the shed.

"Does Chip look different to you?" asked Ginny. "He looks fatter, even longer. The spots aren't there, and his tail doesn't look the same."

The next time Chip ran to the birdfeeder, Ivy snapped a picture of him with her cell phone. To both the women's surprise, it wasn't Chip the chipmunk.

It turned out to be a rat. Maybe a pregnant one.

"How can I have rats?" Ginny exclaimed. "I'm so clean and careful with my garbage. I pick up everything in the backyard, and my home is clean. How is this possible?"

"Mom, Doug Randall, the slumlord, next door has his tenants' garbage over the hillside. Their dumpster has a hole in the bottom. I've urged you to complain to the blight officer and the mayor. Seagulls eat three meals a day there. Now will you listen to me?"

The next morning Ginny called a pest control company, the blight officer, and the health department. The pest control company came right out to survey the problem. They installed big black boxes they called "kill boxes" behind her fence, saying that should take care of the rats. There would be a fee for the service. It upset Ginny because she would harm these animals in the process, even if they were rats.

The blight officer, Carter Dawson, a retired police officer, had an appointment for nine at Ginny's house.

Ginny was waiting for him.

"Hello, I'm Carter Dawson, the blight officer. I understand that you have a rat problem."

She explained her dilemma concerning the rats, garbage, and the overgrowth on the hilltop. The health department never got back to her.

Carter took out his cell phone and tapped in a number. "Hi, Senator, how are you? I need you to light a fire under the health department's feet. I'm standing here with this gracious lady with rats." He smiled at Ginny, his wide brown eyes sparkling. She blushed. He gave the person on the other end her address. "Well, that should take care of that."

Ginny was impressed but cautious. A few sympathetic words wouldn't sway her. "Thank you," she responded.

As they strolled toward Carter's vehicle. A car drove into the driveway. It was Barton Stanton, the mayor of the city. "This is becoming amusing," thought Ginny. "Why the mayor?"

"Why Ginny Adams, such a ruckus over a few Norway rats," the mayor chuckled. "They are prevalent in this neighborhood."

"That's funny. That's not what the pest control person informed me. He told me he hadn't been out in this neighborhood in years for these so-called Norway rats."

"What do you want me to do?" the mayor asked.

Ginny looked straight into his face and answered, "The job we elected you to do. Not for some, but every taxpayer. The Randall family has bullied the citizens of the city for years. Doug Randall has made the apartments next to me a slum. It's a disgrace to the neighborhood."

The mayor's chubby face turned red. Ginny noticed the throbbing veins in his neck and his tight-lipped smile. He was furious.

"I'm doing the best job I can, Ginny," the mayor chided, sweat pouring down his plump face. The perspiration soaked his shirt. "Why was he so nervous? Or maybe it's just because he was so damned overweight," thought Ginny.

"Well, I'll figure it out on my own and put an end to it. I think there's more to this rat case than meets the eye," said Ginny.

With that, the mayor stormed away, getting into his car and backing down the driveway.

"Have an enjoyable day!" yelled Ginny at the moving car.

Carter Dawson left after the mayor.

She took a stroll around her property to examine her lavish flower beds and clear her head. Anna Bishop, a neighbor from the condos behind her, came out to talk to her.

Anna, a widow, had lived in the condos for years. She was in her seventies, with a creamy complexion and a gentle manner. "I noticed those rats in your backyard from my upstairs window. They've been behind our condos for a few years. Remember, the barn and business building on the property?" she asked.

"I do," replied Ginny.

"Well, when the current owners knocked down the old barn and the electric repair building, there were rats everywhere. They have kill boxes on the property like yours," she said. "There was something odd about that transaction."

"In what way?" asked Ginny.

"The landowner didn't want to sell. Then he disappeared. He owed thousands of dollars in back taxes. Everyone figured he just left town. The city sold the property to anonymous buyers. They also, purchased the docks across the street and land behind the condos. It sold for two million dollars. So, you know they have serious plans," Anna told Ginny.

Ginny was so intrigued by this information. Why hadn't anyone mentioned those rats, and the kill boxes on this property? The rats must have run out of food and moved next door to the dumpster, then down to her backyard.

Leashing her two dogs, Ginny took off for some exploring. The property had a "Do Not Enter" sign, but Ginny ignored it. She entered anyway. The old trees bordered the land, acting as guards. They muffled the sound of the traffic on the street, creating a peaceful haven for the creatures that lived inside. The dogs pulled hard on their leashes, determined to rush up the hill. But she spotted the black kill boxes in the overgrowth. Maggie, her Yorkie, tugged hard on her leash. It slipped out of Ginny's hand, and Maggie rushed into the wooded field. Running after her, Ginny let go of Oscar's leash.

Soon Maggie appeared with an object in her mouth. Ginny grabbed her and pried it out of her mouth. A bone. Ginny was positive it was human. Her blue eyes just stared at it in horror. The missing owner's bone, perhaps? Getting her phone out, she dialed 911. The police arrived within minutes.

The officer got out of his car and walked over to Ginny and the dogs.

"You know this is private property. It's posted," he said.

The officer resembled a high school student. Ginny stared at him. "I'm trying to find proof of rats and to see if they are coming from here."

"Where do you live?" he asked.

"In the grey house right over there," She said. "Norway rats will go three-hundred feet from the burrows. That's about the distance from here to my house."

"I'm sorry about the rats, but this doesn't give you the right to trespass."

He no sooner got those words out, and the mayor drove up.

"Do you always answer 911 calls?" Ginny asked.

Perspiration ran down his reddish face as usual. He was furious about Ginny being there.

"What the hell were you thinking? Intruding on private property, snooping around, and releasing your dogs? You might end up with a steep fine or jail time," he said with anger in his voice.

"You're overreacting," said Ginny. "Or do you have an interest or stake in this property?" The way you're acting, one might get that impression."

He didn't acknowledge the questions.

Next, the medical examiner drove on to the property. He got out of his car and strolled over to Ginny. "Can I have the evidence, please?"

"First, I have a few questions," said Ginny. "When will I know if the bone is human, male or female? How long has the bone been here?

His eyes widened. "You're who? Why do I have to deal with your questions?"

"I am a taxpayer, and I pay your salary." With that, she handed him the bone.

The police taped off the area and searched for other evidence. They ordered Ginny and the dogs to go home and stay there.

Ginny rushed home. She dashed up the deck stairs and into the safety of her house. Tears trickling down her face. Had she and the dogs discovered a crime? Was she in danger? She called Ivy to come to the house. Ivy drove as fast as she could to her mom's home.

"Mom, what's so important that I had to rush over here?" Ivy asked.

Ginny told her the entire story and how concerned she was. Ivy was furious at her mother for inspecting the property.

Suddenly, a long, wailing scream and red and blue flashing lights raced up Ginny's driveway. A tall thin curly-haired police officer got out on the operator's side. Another large- framed bald officer emerged from the passenger's side.

Ivy sprang to her feet and ran out the door. Ginny was not far behind. The two officers were climbing the stairs of the deck.

"What is going on?" asked Ivy.

"We need to question Mrs. Adams," the officer responded.

"Was the commotion with the squad car necessary?" asked Ginny.

Ivy glared at the officers.

"Mrs. Adams, we need to take your statement on what transpired today when you discovered the bone."

They asked several questions, and she explained what had taken place and how the dogs had gotten loose. The heavy-set officer wrote on his notepad.

"Are you going to arrest me," asked Ginny.

"It's up to the property owners," replied the officer.

"Have you identified who they are?" asked Ginny.

"It's a group of people, some LLC," he answered.

"How will I know if there are any charges?"

The officer's phone vibrated. He glanced at the screen. "You're in luck. The property owners won't be pressing charges. But you have to stop going over there, or they will charge you with criminal trespassing. Understand?"

"My mother understands," said Ivy, not giving her mother a chance to answer.

"One more question?" asked Ginny. "When will I find out if the bone is human?"

"I can't answer that question." With that, they got up and left.

"Mom, let this one go," said Ivy. "There may have been a murder of someone on that property. The owners could be anybody. Please promise me you won't play detective anymore."

"I promise to stay off the property. But I will find out who owns it," said Ginny.

Up early the next morning, Ginny got onto her computer. She realized that the information she was searching for would be available on the internet. But what search engine to use? She started with Google. Then the phone rang, interrupting her search.

"Hello," said Ginny.

"Hi, this is Officer Cummings," the voice responded on the other end. "I've taken over the case of The Blue Waterway Company, where you and the dogs located the bone. Just making sure you're following orders to stay off it."

"I'm not a child," replied Ginny. "Thank you for checking in with me." She hung up the phone and smiled. He had identified the company.

Ginny got back on her computer and typed in The Blue Waterway Company on the State of Connecticut's site. It popped right up with the identities of the associates. Ginny was not shocked who the owners were. She called her daughter.

"You will never believe who owns that property," said Ginny.

"Who is it?" Ivy asked.

"The mayor, Barton Stanton the slumlord, Doug Randall, and the blight officer Carter Dawson. They propose to develop expensive townhouses and dockominiums. You know, it's the water-based version of a condominium. That means millions of dollars for them," said Ginny.

"Mom, don't tell anybody what you found out. Not even the police. Understand?" said Ivy. "You might be in danger."

"Danger! What kind of danger?" replied Ginny.

"Remember, you turned up a bone on their property. People have murdered for less. Just don't tell anyone. I'll be there soon," said Ivy.

A clicking noise on her phone told her someone was calling.

"Hello," said Ginny.

"I gave you the Blue Waters name. They own the property. Please don't make it public until we identify the bone," said the officer.

"Okay, I will keep it to myself," said Ginny. She already told Ivy, but he didn't need to know that. Ginny wondered if it wasn't public knowledge, anyway.

The screen door opened, and Ivy appeared, panting from running up the deck stairs and rushing over to her mother's house. Before Ivy caught her breath, Ginny blurted out what the officer had told her. Ivy started sobbing.

"Please don't cry," Ginny said. "I won't tell anyone what I found out. I promise."

The phone rang. The caller identification announced it was the local newspaper. Ginny didn't answer. They left a message.

"Hi, Mrs. Adams. I wonder if you would care to comment on the bone you and your dog found. The medical examiner's office told us it belongs to a male missing person. It shows he must have eaten a rabbit or something that ingested the poison in the boxes. The police are looking for more evidence on the property. It's an ongoing investigation. Please call me if you would like to comment. Thanks."

"I can't believe it. I'm so glad it's not the former landowner," sighed Ginny.

"What do you mean the former owner?" asked Ivy.

Ginny told Ivy what Anne had told her. He just vanished, and the property was sold for back taxes. She had hoped the bone she found wasn't his.

"The blight officer, the mayor, and the slumlord have been covering up their plans for a while now," said Ginny. "The rats changed that when they appeared in my backyard. They assumed no one would investigate the property. The rat trail leads right back to the three of them."

The phone rang. It was Anna Bishop, the friend from the condos. "The police and cadaver dogs are roaming the property behind me. Call me."

Ginny started for the door.

"Mom, stop!" yelled Ivy.

Ginny ran out the door, her daughter's voice an echo in her ears. She dashed to the edge of the property. The police wouldn't let her go any further.

"What's going on here?" Ginny asked.

"They discovered a skeleton," the officer replied.

"Do you have any idea who?"

"No, it's premature to say," answered the officer.

Ginny felt in her heart that it was Derek Austin, the former landowner. He must not have wanted to sell to the Blue Waterway owners. One or all of the owners killed him. She couldn't see them as murders, but wealth causes people do peculiar things.

As she made her way home, she reflected how the rats had affected everyone's life. Greed had driven these men to choose material wealth, authority, or fame. Ginny believed that you reap what you sow. She wondered if the money and the power made them feel better. Now his killers would suffer the actions of their greed. Karma.

THE MAN IN THE DARK

Grace opened the back door, walked out onto the deck, and drew in the picturesque moment as the sun rose. Warm colors filled the sky and painted the earth below, producing small ripples of excitement in the river. She watched and let the breeze wash over her, taking in the smell of a new day. Grace tied her black-brown dachshund, Oliver, to his run and gazed out at the train station lights across the river. Darkness was fading and, while it did, the night's blackness rubbed off. On the horizon, yellow rays of light clawed their way skyward. Night fled, but she didn't care. A new day was about to start.

She heard a roar in the distance. Was it thunder? Turning her head slightly toward the sound, the roar became louder and louder. A chugging and the blast of a horn followed it. Such a mournful sound. The brakes hissed and screeched as the train approached to the station. A voice barked over the loudspeaker, "Boston on track one, New York on track two!"

Grace smiled to herself, untied Oliver, and went into the house. Grace was a woman in the autumn of her life. She had taken care of her parents until their death and never married.

Inheriting the waterfront property, she now worked from home for several computer companies. Makeup couldn't hide her wrinkle lines. Still, there was strength and wisdom in her emerald green eyes.

She worked in the dark on her computer. Oliver barked at something outside the window. Grace tried quieting him down, but he wouldn't have it. She peered out the window. A man was picking bottles out of bins at each house and putting them into a big black plastic bag. With the bag and the bike, he maneuvered himself to Grace's driveway. He lifted her bin. The incessant barking of the dog startled him. He was tall and slim and a dark hooded sweatshirt covered his face.

He glanced around to discover where the barking was coming from. Frightened, Grace slipped lower into the recliner, even though the dark hid her. She crawled along the floor and grabbed Oliver off the couch, quieting him. When she peeked over the windowsill, she saw that the man was in the funeral parlor parking lot next to her house. He appeared to be searching for something in front of the funeral home door. The lighting was inadequate, so she couldn't identify what he was doing.

"I'll check it out later," Grace thought to herself.

At ten o'clock Oliver and Grace left for their daily walk to the park at the end of the street. On the way back, Grace and Oliver took a minor detour to the funeral parlor parking lot. She wanted to see if she could find out what the hooded man had been looking for. What Grace discovered was a large, black plastic smoker's receptacle for cigarette butts. Removing the cover on the bin, she found many more cigarette butts stuffed inside a silver pail. The man on the bike must have been searching for cigarettes that hadn't burned to the end. Perhaps he didn't have money for them, and that's why he collected cans. She looked at a piece of paper sticking out from underneath the pail. Grace grabbed it. As she did, a car pulled into the lot. Grace recognized the driver as one of the funeral directors. She stuffed the note into her pocket. Oliver barked at the car and then began wagging his tail.

"Taking up smoking, Grace?" laughed Franklin, the funeral director.

"No," she replied, embarrassed. "I never noticed this before. A man this morning was rummaging through it. I was a little curious."

So, you're playing detective again?" laughed Franklin.

"Just a little," she responded.

"See that red flashing light in the corner? It's a camera," said Franklin.

Grace smiled, but inside she was panicking. Was she on the camera stealing the note she had in her pocket?

Franklin sensed she was nervous. "Truth is the camera isn't pointed correctly, and we can only see certain movements." With that, he opened the funeral parlor door and excused himself. He didn't mention the truth about the camera. It could see everything happening in the lot. But why make her feel apprehensive or even suspicious of what was going on in the funeral home?

Grace let out a deep sigh as she entered the house. She would have to wait until later, or even tomorrow, to return the note she had in her pocket. Besides, she hadn't even read it yet.

When she got inside, she took the paper out and read it: "Red Sox and Yankees, 4:00 PM rush hour, time to play the game at the station."

Grace took out her phone and snapped a picture of the note. She waited until everyone had left the parking lot and crept down, putting the note under the smoker pail where she had taken it. Then, she hustled back to the house and bolted the doors.

"What did it all mean?" Grace kept asking herself that question as she cooked supper for Oliver and herself. Later that evening, Grace took the dog outside for a quick walk around her property. She glanced down at the vacant lot and at that smoker's bin, hoping there would be another note tomorrow. She loved this adventure and referred to the hooded prowler as Bike Man. Her life could use a little excitement.

The next morning, Grace waited in the dark in her chair for Bike Man to come. He didn't disappoint her. For three more days, he showed up at the same time. Each day she would walk down to the funeral home parking lot and take a picture of the note about the game at the train station. Then she would put it back. She wondered if this man realized she had been reading his notes and what he would do about it.

On the fourth day, he didn't show up until later. For the first time, Grace saw his head and face. Besides being tall, he had a full beard and black hair. Bike Man looked familiar, but she couldn't quite place him. Yet, Grace knew she had seen him before.

As she watched him, he turned around and stared straight at her house. She leaned back from the window, frightened. Why had she taken those notes in the first place? Why had she continued reading them? Maybe someone was playing a game with her, or perhaps someone was planning to create mischief at the train station. Confused and scared, Grace called her old friend Irene from high school.

"Hello, this is Irene."

"Hi, it's Grace. Can I come over and chat with you?"

"Is anything wrong?" asked Irene.

"I'm not sure," replied Grace.

"How is one o'clock?" asked Irene.

"Great, see you then," said Grace.

Grace drove to Irene's house just before one o'clock. Irene greeted her, and they went into the house. Irene, sixty-two years old, had short grey hair and a plump middle-aged shaped frame. Grace explained the story and showed the photographs of the notes on her phone. Irene, a retired federal agent, still kept in contact with her former coworkers. While Irene made the calls, Grace waited.

"You'll have visitors in a few days, if not sooner. Don't continue searching for the notes and stay away from the parking lot!" ordered Irene. Grace thanked her and drove home.

As she pulled onto her street, she noticed there was a party going at a house on the opposite side. Guests were standing on the deck and strolling around the yard. Then she recognized him: Bike Man. At the party! Or did he live there? Is that why he looked so familiar?

Bike Man stared at her. Her heart began thumping hard, like it might burst right out of her chest. "Calm down," she thought. "You can't let him realize you recognize him." She got out of her car and darted into the house. Fear washed over her. Grace's hands began sweating. Her breathing quickened along with her heart rate.

The doorbell rang. Oliver began his incessant barking. Who could it be? Was Bike Man outside her door? Had he come to confront her because of the notes? Or worse, was he planning on harming her because of what he thought she knew? Grace stared out her window. No cars in her driveway. She panicked. Should she rush out the front door? The doorbell rang again. Grace walked to the back door and peered through the glass window. There stood two suited men. She waited a moment and gathered herself. The bell rang again. She cleared her throat.

"Did Irene send you?" Grace asked through the door.

"Yes," they said.

She asked for their shields. Both men held up their badges to the glass window so Grace could see they were United States Marshals. Opening the door, she requested their picture identification. She invited them into the house. Oliver growled and smelled the men. They both wielded an air of authority.

"You should never have taken those notes," said the younger, lean marshal. "You've put yourself in grave danger."

"But now that you have, we'd like you to help us capture him," he continued. "Can we stay the night?"

"Why?" asked Grace.

"We want to look at him in action," said the older, grey-haired marshal.

Her heart pounded like the thrumming wings of a caged bird. "Why me?" she asked herself. Why hadn't she just minded her own business? "Playing detective again," echoed in her head.

"What if I say no?" asked Grace.

"We'll figure out another way," the younger marshal said. "Is that what you want?"

"No, you can stay," Grace replied.

They took up their posts. Each marshal took a turn sleeping on the sofa.

In the morning, Grace remained at her computer, performing as she did every day in case someone was watching the house. As she worked, Oliver began barking.

Sure enough, there was Bike Man.

He went right to the smoker's bin. To his amazement, there was a full pack of cigarettes. He hesitated and then put the note in the bin. Grace took a picture of and showed it to the marshals. As they looked at the note, their faces tensed, and they glanced at each other. She knew it was urgent.

"Please let me read it," Grace asked. It said: "Friday rush hour 4:00 PM. I'll hit a home run."

"What does that mean?" asked Grace.

"It sounds like he's ready to attack the train station," answered the younger marshal, running his hands through his messy brown hair.

"But today is Wednesday," replied Grace with a disturbed tone in her voice.

"We must move fast. Will you help us?" he asked.

"What can I do?" answered Grace.

"You are the only one who knows what this guy looks like," he said.

"But if I help you, my life could be over. He'll learn who told!" blurted out Grace.

We have a plan to help you with that. Do you trust us?" he asked.

"Do I have a choice?" asked Grace.

"You could say no. But if something takes place, how are you going to feel?" the older marshal said. "Passengers at the train station could die. Do you want that on your conscience?"

Grace knew she could never live with herself if she said no. She agreed to help them, and they went to work on their plan. It took Wednesday and Thursday to get everything in place. On Friday afternoon, they left Grace's house for the train station at 3:00 PM.

At 4:00 PM, Grace appeared on the train platform with all the other people waiting. She surveyed the faces of the crowd. Then Grace saw Franklin, the funeral director. She signaled the marshals and wandered over to him.

"Going someplace, Franklin?" asked Grace. "Or maybe you're waiting for some explosive coffins," she taunted.

Franklin grinned at her. Then a serious expression came over his face.

"You shouldn't be such a snoop, Grace," he said. "But you're too late to do anything."

Franklin put one hand inside his coat. But as he did, an arm slipped around his neck with a pistol positioned at his head.

"Take your hand out of your coat!" ordered a deep voice holding the gun.

Grace glanced in the voice's direction. It was Bike Man, the guy she had spied on for weeks.

"You're a marshal?" asked Grace.

"No, Homeland Security," answered Bike Man, winking at her.

Franklin was on the ground, cuffed, and being read his rights. Grace realized this must have been a sting operation, and she had gotten herself in the middle of it. She thought Bike Man was the person the marshals were searching for, and they had let her believe that, so Franklin would show up at the train station. But she was still in danger from Franklin's partners and had to be protected from harm.

The marshals had promised Grace they had a method to manage her safety. They escorted her to a black automobile. The door opened, and there was Oliver and her suitcase. The blue-suited man inside gestured for her to join him, and the door closed behind her.

He handed her a large envelope with her new identity. The Marshalls had told her this was the only way she would be safe from harm. She opened it and took out the papers. Grace had a new name, a new home, and a new state to live in. Even Oliver had a new name. Grace was now Ursula Clark. Oliver was now Oscar. They had not been so imaginative with his name. She realized her life as she knew it was over. Because Grace had gathered the notes and sensed a crime was being plotted, she had saved many lives. Hers had been altered forever.

THE WATER WHISPER

Shell pink and gold tints decorated the sky as daylight burst over the Connecticut River. Maggie Lord sat on her deck drinking her third mug of coffee, staring at the night still battling with the sunlight. These sleepless nights had become fewer since her move from New York City two weeks ago to an over fifty-five society in a modest waterfront town. Her condo was still without drapes, and several unpacked boxes and unhung clothing needed a closet.

Maggie's doctors advised her to take it slow. Her wounds from her last undercover assignment came close to taking her life. She'd been a narcotics enforcement officer for twenty years in New York. It had been hectic but she loved it. It was time to open a new chapter in her life. But she missed the hustle and bustle of the city.

Trying to move her leg to adjust herself, Maggie's cat Hector glanced up at her with his golden eyes and yawned. Hector was a solid grey cat from the top of his nose to the tip of his tail, including his whiskers. He loved to curl up with Maggie and purr loudly. He remained by Maggie's side during her recovery and never let her move very far out of his sight. She padded his head and then made her way to standing with intense pain in her limbs. A breeze came off the water blowing her salt and pepper hair and her night clothing that hung over her skinny frame.

As she stood there attempting to get her balance, she over-heard voices. The people next door? Maggie heard it again. Perhaps someone's television? The voices were unclear, but she thought she heard the words "drugs" and "informer".

She laughed out loud and told herself, "You're not in law enforcement anymore." Walking back into the condo, the cat watched her, and she hoped for a few hours of sleep.

All day long, Maggie thought about what she had heard. It was haunting her. She went onto the deck several times and listened. It was hard to hear anything because of all the noise. There was construction, trucks operating in of the neighborhood and hammers banging on the new condos. The river traffic, with tug boats traveling up and down and the train station across the water, made it all more challenging to hear anything.

The station was an old red brick building with dark wood trim. She struggled to image what it looked like inside. Were there homeless people sleeping on the heater grates? Drug dealers making deals? Or prostitutes turning tricks? Every individual in the station had a story—somewhere they're heading and some-thing that's important to them. The voices couldn't have come from there. Could they?

During the next weeks, her neighbors dropped by and intro-duced themselves, asking if she needed any help. Maggie asked them if they ever heard voices early in the dawn. They gave her a peculiar look and then pointed out how sound carried on the water. Plus, the train station across the river, you picked up strange noises and voices. Maggie thought that's what she must have heard.

The new place kept her busy for several weeks and she was so exhausted she collapsed into bed. Then another sleepless night. She dreamt of her old police job, being shot by the gang leader and slipping into the depths of drugs and alcohol hell. Maggie made coffee. She preferred a scotch on the rocks. She had been sober for six months. Coffee would now be her drink of choice. She went out onto the deck and savored her coffee.

There it was, those two voices again. "The squealer has to go."

"I didn't bargain for this," a soft, high-pitched chirp said.

"If we don't do it, he'll do it to us," a low male voice answered.

In the background, Maggie heard the station attendant calling out the tracks for the trains. She heard the train whistles coming closer. The brakes hissed and wheels screech as the trains slowed and they approached the station.

"Boston on Track One, New York on Track Two," announced the voice over the loudspeaker.

She was in a quandary about what to do. Maybe this wasn't what she thought it was. Maybe she wasn't as well as she thought she was. Maggie needed to talk to someone she knew and trusted. But who? She didn't know anyone here that she could discuss this with. "What about my old partner," she thought, "Mason Barkley?"

"Homicide," Detective Barkley replied on the phone.

"Mason, it's me, Maggie."

"What's up, pretty lady?" Mason replied with a chuckle.

"I need your help."

Mason and Maggie had been partners for many years. They'd had always had each other's back. When she got shot and took her journey into drugs and alcohol, he had reported her to the chief. She had been drunk or on pills often on duty. Mason had become concerned for her safety and his own. They had a falling out, and when she left for Connecticut, they weren't talking.

Maggie thought about Mason's sandy-blonde hair and his piercing blue eyes, the color of the ocean. He was handsome, and she missed him. Mason always made Maggie smile and laugh with his corny jokes and the look in his blue eyes. When he talked, it was mesmerizing.

"What do you need, pretty lady?" he laughed, hoping she wasn't in trouble again.

Maggie sensed a hesitation in his voice.

"I'm still sober," she whispered.

"I know."

"I'm coming into New York City on Friday. Can you meet me for lunch?" Maggie asked.

"Friday," Mason replied.

"I'll call when I'm finished with my appointment."

She took the train early to New York and went to her doctor's appointment. Maggie then called Mason. "Meet me at Frank's at noon."

"Okay," Mason replied.

Frank's was a place they had gone for lunch many times as partners. Mason arrived at noon and Maggie was in their usual booth. They hugged and exchanged small talk. It was strained. Maggie put her hand on Mason's.

"Thank you for caring," she said. "I was in a dark place and I could have gotten both of us killed. You were brave to turn me in. I would be dead if it wasn't for you."

Tears rolled down Mason's face. "Maggie, thanks for telling me that. I hoped you didn't hate me. Tell me what you need."

"I think I heard two or more people planning a drug deal," said Maggie. Mason knew her well enough to know that if she was suspicious something was going on.

"I have a contact with law enforcement where you live. Lieutenant Dalton. I'll call him and have him contact you."

"Thank you. I knew I could depend on you."

They hugged and Maggie left for the train.

The next time she heard the voices, she recorded them. That way she could listen to them again during the day. She wanted to figure out what they were discussing. Was it a crime? Maybe it was a program they watched? In today's world, it could be anything.

After several recordings she recognized that whatever the two people were planning it would on a Friday morning. It wasn't obvious which train they were targeting, New York or Boston. She hadn't figured that part of the puzzle out yet. She decided that next Friday she would be on the train platform to discover if she could figure out who the voices were on her recordings. She knew she was searching for a male with a low and flat voice and female that had a high-pitched voice. "That narrows it down," she thought and laughed out loud.

Friday morning, Maggie was up and out of the house by five. She parked her car and made her way to the train station. As she entered the station, there were homeless people sleeping by the heating registers. She got tense and a bead of perspiration appeared on her forehead. Looking around at the people, she spotted a guy with tattoos edging up his neck. "Gang member," Maggie thought, as she glanced at him. Tattoos on the neck, head or face was an immediate red flag. He peered at her and gave her a wink. She turned away. He couldn't possibly know who she was. She had covered her tracks by moving out of the city to this place. It was a flashback to her old detective's job she told herself.

The ticket agent called out the trains and what track. People were stirring, shuffling their feet and glancing around at their fellow passengers. Is it time? Maggie walked over to the platform to survey the people boarding. There wasn't no one that fit the profile she had developed in her head.

The train door behind her opened, making a cracking noise. Two police officers stepped onto the platform. Their eyes met Maggie's. She smiled at them. Should she tell them what she was doing there? Would they believe her? If they checked her past, they would find out she had been a detective in New York City, that a high-ranking drug lord had shot her during an arrest, and that she lost her way into alcohol and drugs to ease the pain of her wounds. Police officers knew that addiction had destroyed lives. Would they believe she had faced her demons and turned her life around? Maggie walked away. She drove home sobbing. "This is recklessness," she thought. "I shouldn't be focusing on this. I should enjoy my new life."

Hector, Maggie's cat, was perched on the deck. Maggie talked to him. He was such an excellent audience and jointly they seemed to iron out problems. The phone rang, disturbing they talk.

"Hello, Maggie Lord."

"Hi, Maggie. I'm Lieutenant Dalton, Mason's acquaintance. I understand you need my help. Let's meet tomorrow at the coffee shop near the train station at ten."

"Perfect," said Maggie.

She was on time, and so was Lieutenant Dalton. She wondered how he knew Mason. He had weather-beaten skin, heavy-hooded brown eyes, a stubbly beard and a portly body. Not at all like Mason. He sensed her surprise. Maggie's presence also surprised him. He had investigated her and knew she had faced dark demons of drugs and alcohol. Mason had also disclosed her serious wounds.

"Let's sit down and talk about what you think you heard," he said.

Maggie took a deep breath. "Two people are plotting to do another person harm on a Friday morning at the train station. I don't know what Friday, but I believe it is about drugs. It sounds bizarre, and you definitely checked me out. I'm not drinking or taking drugs."

He reached across the table and took Maggie's hand. "I'm here for information, not judgment," he said.

Maggie teared up. She got herself under control.

"I know you have been through a lot and have fought your way back. This has nothing to do with that. We have a serious heroin problem in this town. There are several gangs and corruption in the ranks of the police department. Several officers have gone to prison along with gang members. I've even been a suspect," he said.

Maggie's mouth dropped open, and she stared in disbelief. Was she sharing this information with the right person?

He could see her uneasiness by the look on her face.

"How would you like to help me out with this?" he asked.

"Me?" said Maggie surprised. "What can I do?"

"You can be my ears. The next time you hear the two voices you need to call me on my cell phone. I'll give you surveillance equipment. Nothing obvious. How does that sound?" he replied.

Maggie nodded. Her heart started beating faster in her chest. Had she done the right thing? "Yes, you can do this," she thought.

She got up several mornings early. No voices. Had they changed their mind and decided not to do what they were planning? Or was Dalton part of this and they had changed their meeting place? Then it happened. She heard the two voices. The day was today. "That can't be right," she thought. "It's not Friday."

Maggie panicked and called the Lieutenant. His phone went to voice mail. She tried several times. Her hands shook. "I need something," her inner voice screamed. "A drink or a pill. No!"

Somehow Maggie got herself together. She grabbed her service revolver and got into her car and drove to the train station. She bolted out of the car and dashed to the station. She was breathless when she got to the platform. Lieutenant Dalton was there with two other officers. One was A slim-hipped female officer and the other was a thick-necked male officer. There weren't any people on the platform. She walked up to Dalton. He stepped away for the officers to talk to her.

The two offices smiled at her. She realized they had been the ones the last time she was on the platform.

As the female officer walked away, she turned and said, "Ellis, see you back at the station."

"Okay," he replied.

"Your name is Ellis?" said Maggie in an alarmed voice.

"Yes," he replied.

"You're the target!" Maggie yelled.

Maggie saw the female officer draw her weapon. She drew hers and got off several rounds. One round hit her in the shoulder. The pain was agonizing. The two officers wore bullet-proof vests. A round knocked the male officer off his feet. Maggie turned to look at Lieutenant Dalton, blood flowing down her arm. He drew his gun.

"Why didn't you shoot?" Maggie yelled at him.

He looked at her with his dark brown eyes. "Because you're the mark, Maggie. There are people who don't need cops like you in their community. They call you the Water Whisper!" he said as he fired.

Maggie fell onto the platform. In the distance she heard sirens coming closer and closer. The bright lights flashed and people yelled. It was Mason's voice. Or was it? Maggie tried to get up, pushing herself to her knees. She felt pressure on her back forcing her back down. Someone's foot? In her blurred vision, she saw a tattoo man. Or did she? Was she back in New York City, being shot again? Or was she dying?

THE MISSION PROJECT

Jennifer Parker's image in the mirror had been her most reliable support, the one individual she could count on. Staring into the mirror, it wasn't about her long, fuzzy, blonde hair or her mysterious green eyes. It was about who she had grown into. She had given up a promising career as a computer game designer to become a wife and mother. She'd been positive that it was the correct decision. But now she sought more, and she recognized she desired to do something about it.

The children now grown, she wanted to go back to her former career. Her husband, Brent, would chuckle at her and say that she had it made. Jen wanted a career in game design, not a life of having it made. "Quit thinking and get ready for tonight," she thought. "Saturday night. Poker Night."

Jen hated poker, as did the other four women who would be there. The men won and never let them forget it. "Whatever happened to sportsmanship?" she wondered. But tonight, would be different, and she wasn't proud of what the women had planned to do. Yet these men deserved a payback.

"Let's go. We'll be late," Brent said, interrupting her thoughts.

Brent was a geek. That's what was appealing to Jen. His web pages and game designs had been profitable and made it possible for her to stay at home with her children and enjoy a remarkable way of life.

He was tall, but not tall enough to be lanky. Brent had a look of confidence etched into his features and into his walk. His fair complexion furthered the striking effect that his auburn hair and amber eyes had on everyone he met. She loved him, but he was suffocating her.

"I'll be right there," she answered. She took one last glance at herself in the mirror and winked.

"Are you ready to lose to the guys tonight?" laughed her husband.

"What an ass," Jen thought. "If only he knew that they had been scheming to whip them tonight."

"The night is young," replied Jen with a chuckle in her voice.

Everybody was at the Douglas' home when they arrived, and the guys were ready to play. The other couples were seated at the olive-green rustic poker table. Men against women. Never couples. The women had suggested a couples' game, but because the women played so poorly, the men didn't want that. So, as usual, the women grinned at each other and played as they had. After the third hand, the assault got underway.

The women had created individual signals. They would lift one finger, blink twice, brush a strand of hair behind their ears, and arrange their chips to convey when to bet and when to fold. They started winning, and it stunned the men. The men battled hard to overcome the winning. They would check when it was their turn. If that didn't work out, they folded. The women were unstoppable. To add to the irritation they were inflicting, they chattered and giggled, upsetting the men. They concluded the game, but not without one last dig.

"How does it feel to lose guys?" The women laughed.

They laughed it off and huddled away from the women next to the foodstuff and booze.

"Well, ladies," said Jen. "I predict we won't be having poker night for a while." They laughed, which got the men's attention, and they peered over at them.

"Just because you got lucky once doesn't mean that will happen again."

"How about a rematch," replied Jen?

The men fired back with ridiculous excuses about how it was becoming late, and they were tired. Then out of the blue, the host, Art Douglas, said. "How about tomorrow instead of your hen party?"

The women got together at each other's house most Sundays and coordinated what they would do for charity functions for their town. When their children were younger, it was carpools and sports. Now that their children were off to college or living on their own, they managed various charity boards. Jen was the one that did the computer design work.

When the men got together, they talked about work, sports, or video games. They were always struggling to out-do each another. The newer the game, the bigger the rivalry.

"Art, we don't have hen parties. We create a better place for our community," said Jen, irritated.

"On that note, it's time to go," said Brent.

He learned not to get on Jen's wrong side, and Art was approaching that.

"Tomorrow, ladies, one o'clock at my home," Jen called out as Brent and she left.

"I can't believe you women beat the hell out of us tonight," said Brent on the ride home. "It's like you had secret signals or something."

"Can't we win? Or do you consider us too dumb to do that?" snapped Jen. She was struggling not to sound defensive or laugh out loud.

"You know, I don't consider you women stupid, but you're terrible at poker. Then tonight you win all but three hands? Well, it's suspicious," he answered.

They pulled into their driveway. Jen got out and went right into the house. She felt miserable. She had never cheated at anything, but this was payback night. The men looked like a train had struck them.

"Coming to bed?" Jen called to Brent.

"I'll be up in a minute. I want to see if I can get to the next level in this game."

Jen knew what that meant. It would be a few hours before he came to bed. If only she could figure out a way to beat him at a video game. Or better, create one he had never considered. "A thought for another time," as she drifted off to sleep.

The next day the women arrived at one o'clock, and each had a dish of food to share. The conversation drifted to the poker game and how enjoyable it had felt to win.

"We need to keep this winning streak going," said Pam.

Pam was Art's wife. They had hosted the game last night. She was a computer nerd and worked at the military base. She had wide brown eyes and curly brown hair. Pam could laugh at herself and find humor in several situations.

"How?" they asked.

"Let's figure out something the men want to do but haven't yet," said Pam.

"You notice how they're always joking? How easy it would be to enter the military base and take control of the gaming activity there. We can do that. That's something the guys would never think of," Jen chimed in.

"Like?" they asked.

"Kidnap Pam's supervisor?" teased Jen.

"The Commander?" Pam gasped.

"Why not?" laughed Jen.

"I don't know what you have been smoking, but that's the craziest idea you've come up with," said Pam.

"Then each one of you come up with a better payback plan, and we will talk about next Sunday. Make sure you concentrate on the details of your plan and how to execute it. You'll have a week."

They left all promising to work on an idea to share next Sunday.

Jen worked hard the whole week on developing and constructing the kidnap game. Hoping the ladies wouldn't change their minds or, worse, think she was deranged. Jen had worked so hard on developing this scheme; that it had turned into a vivid fictional world in her mind. She talked to herself about stuff that would emerge, like which of the women would perform what part and how long each sequence would take. Pam, Kate, Janet, and Fran each had a piece of this payback game, as they did in the poker scam. Jen wanted them to have an actual picture of what she was constructing and how important the pieces were in the design.

The group met at Pam's home, and each told what they had produced. Pam wanted another poker game where they didn't crush the men as before. Kate and Janet had designed a water game. It involved kayaking, canoeing, and swimming.

Fran wanted a golf match. Jen's design was the strongest by far. Although they weren't positive they could do it, they agreed to it.

Since Pam worked at the facility as a computer programmer. She would do the dangerous part. She would have to get them on the military base. They broke up the tasks into a format that fairly resembled a motion picture scenario, complete with dialogue and setting. This way, they could design the scenes then put them together. It would offer them a chance to review if they had forgotten anything. Jen would be the team leader because it was her design, and she knew how to write the code for the game. She explained what part of the game each woman had to work on and the plan for getting everything developed.

The following Sunday, they traveled to the place above the base to create a pathway through the thick woods. It was green, thick, and mystical. Sunlight penetrated through the top branches. Decaying leaves produced a crunching sound under their feet. Branches created a snapping noise as they made a pathway to the clearing above the base. The lighting was inadequate, but it would do. They cut the branches that stuck out and hindered them from moving to the observation point. Kate and Janet, the pot-smoking, grey haired artisans of the group would make their way to this location at dawn on the day of the kidnapping. They would be on lookout, to make certain the others sneaked onto the base and slipped out with no trouble. When Pam's van left the base, they would meet back at their proposed rendezvous spot.

Now that they had that part completed, they worked on the essential components. How were they going to get on the base and abduct the commander? Pam recognized there was a sequence to his duty schedule. She went to work at odd hours. The guards at the gate got acquainted with her hours. Then it happened. Pam overheard one of the military men discussing how the commander ran alone on the running track at dawn. "That's it," she thought. "We'll snatch him at the track." She called Jen.

"Hi," said Jen. "What fantastic news do you have for me?"

"I've learned where we can do it," she whispered.

"Great! Let's meet at Harriett's tavern. It's slow tonight, and the guys won't be wondering what we are doing. I'll meet you after work, and we'll chat. I'll call the others," said Jen.

The arrived at seven o'clock at the tavern. The women ordered a pitcher of margaritas, each savoring the first few sips. They all felt the mental stress and nervous tension. They chit-chatted a bit then got to work. Pam explained what she'd learned at the office, about when the commander would be at the track.

"How are we going to get him at the track?" Fran questioned.

Fran the golfer, miss curiosity, thought Jen. She had to have everything spelled out for her. Fran was the tomboy of the group, sporting a short, no-nonsense haircut. Her skin was tan from the hours she'd spent on the golf course.

"If you give me a few days Fran, I'll change the code on the programming," said Jen. "I've got to analyze the data, and I'll make this work."

"I hope so," said Fran. "We have a lot riding on this." I still think the golf tournament is the way to get these guys,

The women glanced at one another and broke into laughter. They played gold as badly as they played poker. The trouble with golf is you can't cheat like they had at poker.

They drained the pitcher and left.

Jen worked on the plan and the timetable to complete the design. She had it figured out by the next meeting. They would meet at the park at 2:30 in the morning. Kate and Janet would go into the woods to the observation point and would bring their cameras. If anyone happened by, they would say they were awaiting the sunrise. The others would leave the park and drive to the gate. Pam would be the driver. Jen and Fran would wait on the van floor hidden. They would drive to the track near Pam's office and hide under the canopy. When the commander neared them, Jen would be on the ground, writhing in pain. Knowing him to be a gentleman, they knew he would stop to help. Then they'd surprise him.

"I'm not positive I can lie on the floor of the van and not budge," said Fran. "I'm just not comfortable with that."

"Just suck it up, Fran," said Jen. "You're the only one complaining."

Now that Jen had the design ready, they all agreed it would be Friday morning. They had a week to make sure everything worked.

The women met at the park, and each took a sip of wine from a bottle Jen had brought. An early victory drink. Pam started the van, and Jen and Fran laid on the floor.

"I am so nervous," said Pam as she approached the gate.

"Getting an early start?" asked the guard.

"I forgot some papers I need for a meeting this morning at another location," replied Pam. Then she drove to her office near the track and parked. Jen and Fran jumped out of the van. They had five minutes to get Jen in position under the canopy and for Fran to hide out of sight. It felt like an eternity to them before they saw the commander. Jen got on the ground and moaned. The commander stopped to help, they overtook him with a rag soaked in chloroform, knocking him out. They had to work fast to haul his limp body into the van. They drove away. Leaving wasn't as challenging as getting in. There were no patrols on the exit side. Pam drove to the rendezvous spot, where the others waited.

The women helped get the commander out of the van and into the hideout. They stopped and looked at each other. The five of them had succeeded. They had done what the men hadn't. They high-five each other and broke out into a celebration. The commander moved. He was disoriented and having trouble breathing.

This wasn't part of the game. An operation must have failed.

"Jen, do something!" shouted the women. She tried several kinds of procedures and codes she knew. "Come on, we are so close," Jen yelled.

In the background, sirens screamed and lights flashed, drawing ever closer. The door to the rendezvous spot flew open, and the women stood there numb. Caught!

"What the hell is going on in here?" their husbands demanded. The five of them were silent. They realized the men had caught them. The five of them had this story created in their heads, which justified their actions. They couldn't admit to themselves their guilt. Wining had taken over them. It had provided them with a feeling of accomplishment, even importance. It gave them a purpose that was being fulfilled. What's wrong for someone else didn't mean it had to be wrong for them.... right? They didn't want to appear weak or unequal to their husbands. If they never went all-in or took a chance, they could never win. They had prevailed on their own. No cheating this time.

Fran, Pam, Janet, and Kate drifted from their positions, and the men could see Jen sitting at the full computer screen. The words "Mission Complete" flashed across the screen in brilliant colors.

Jen broke the silence. "Come on in and join us. We've created, designed, and executed an authentic live-action video game. We just completed the top level. Each of us assumed a role in the game and completed our tasks. The game is called The Mission Project. Care to start on level one?"

THE END